KNUCKLES

KNUCKLES

by

Clarence Budington Kelland

HARPER & BROTHERS *Publishers*
New York *and* London
MCMXXVIII

KNUCKLES

KNUCKLES

CHAPTER I

ASPHALT pavement was the natural heath of the Cross family. Each member of it had been born upon the island of Manhattan, and none of the three ever had climbed a flight of stairs to the bedroom. Each had been born in an apartment, raised in an apartment, and—if they ever gave a thought to the matter—proposed to die in an apartment. Their rise in the world could be traced by the improvement in the quality and size of the apartments they occupied, and their ideal home was an apartment on the Drive overlooking the river. Their ambition was to own such a home—to buy a section of one of those coöperative tenant-owned buildings which should have a marble lobby and a uniformed attendant to open car doors.

Warren Cross, at the age of thirty-two years, held a position which gave promise of better things with the Consolidated Lumber Corporation. He was by way of being efficient at producing efficiency and he rather delighted in encountering chaos that he might reduce it to order. Reducing the overhead was a passion with him.

He was of that slender, trim, meticulously dressed habit which one has come to associate with bank clerks or with the more successful employees of bro-

1

kerage houses. His manner was attractive and his manners pleasing without being obtrusive. Of evenings he seemed to churn with nervous energy, so that when they were not entertaining friends at bridge, or being entertained, he must go out to the movies or to a theater. He loved also to discover new places to dine—little intimate *table d'hôte* places where the food was good and the prices reasonable. The papers and an occasional magazine supplied his reading, and his æsthetic side was more than satisfied by the few symphony concerts and recitals in Carnegie Hall or Æolian Hall to which his wife conducted him.

His wife, Janet, was five years younger than he, slender, and, though not beautiful, the possessor of what Warren called class. She was a wholesome young woman who regretted that their income had not been large enough to have children, and she was very fond of her husband, though sometimes inclined to be brisk in her manner toward him. This, however, was probably her way of showing proprietorship. She was intelligent, understood politics, knew rather more than most people about music, and sang very well with what voice she had. It was not a large voice or a very fine voice, but she was credited with more than she possessed, because her intelligence and appreciation made the most of it.

She was of an economical turn, and though her husband was uniformly delighted with her appearance, he marveled privately at the reasonable cost of her clothing. She was a shopper—a keen shopper—who knew where to go and how to get the best for the least. In common with her husband she appreciated humor and possessed a sunny wit and a flair for the turning of phrases which added materially to her social value.

The third and by no means least important member of the family was Warren's sister Sarah, who had lived with them since the death of her mother some four years before. Sarah was very dark, with beautiful black hair, which she wore short about her admirably shaped head. Hers was one of those pert faces which flashed expressions with bewildering rapidity, and if her mouth was a trifle large, it was no defect, for her teeth were exquisite—almost as exquisite as her legs, which her dresses, always abreast of the mode, made no pretense of concealing. She was a vivid person at whom both men and women turned to look, and she had not the remotest idea what the world was all about—except that it was a splendid, hurrying, scurrying place in which to disport oneself.

Sarah danced. She counted as lost that evening when some young man did not take her to a dancing place. One could hardly say she had a character, for nothing had ever happened to form it. What she would do in any emergency, how she would develop, it was impossible to say. She could be tempestuous, and she could be very patient and self-sacrificing, but one never knew when. But one thing she knew—

and her brother was confident of it as well—she was efficiently able to take care of herself among the younger generation with whom she spent her evenings. She was twenty, and had been too busy to fall in love even very slightly.

Once a week Warren and Janet and Sarah, generally with some young gentleman of her circle, dined out and danced late at a cabaret. They were satisfied with the life, if only they could have a bit more of it. They liked what they did, but looked forward to doing it a little better; no alteration of any kind was ever so much as considered—only an improvement in quality as their income should increase. It was their world; in fact, they believed it was the world; they were unconscious of any other except by vague hearsay which did not arouse their interest. Not only could they not imagine themselves leading another sort of life, but they could not imagine anybody else doing so. They were urban to the innermost fibers of their beings; they were more than urban—they were New Yorkers.

April was dwindling away and the day was Saturday. Warren Cross, wearing a light spring overcoat, walked more slowly than was his custom as he made his progress toward the Subway. His face was unusually grave; had been perturbed since he left the private office of Mr. Dinsmore twenty minutes before. Mr. Dinsmore had summoned him at eleven, and the interview had consumed an hour and a half. . . . Now Warren paused at the corner of Broadway; paused and stared up and down the street almost with the air of a countryman who was seeing it for the first time. He felt a sudden interest in Broadway, a sudden appreciation of it. He was not conscious that he ever had been aware of Broadway before; he had taken it for granted; it was a part of his environment, something to be accepted casually, without thought. The ear may be an important part of one's anatomy, but one is wholly unconscious of its presence until it chooses to ache.

Instead of descending to the Subway, Warren walked northward. It was an impulse; he would walk the four blocks to the next station. But when the next station was reached he still did not descend; he did not wish to abandon that spectacle or cease to hear that clamor. So he continued to walk, block after block—and that though he knew each moment would make later and later his arrival at home. Perhaps that had something to do with it—a reluctance to get home. He found himself in the theater crowd above Fortieth Street and suddenly was aware of the desirability of being there at that time. Times Square! Streets packed with crawling motor-cars! Girls with metropolitan faces, colored stockings! Men blocking the walks by exhibiting mechanical toys! Traffic policemen! Dapper men with walking-sticks and queer-looking old men trying to appear young! Fat women in limousines! Traffic officers blowing whistles! A vortex, a swirl, a composite sound of which the accustomed ear was unconscious

until it concentrated upon listening! New York!
This was the heart of New York, the heart of that
great entity of whose composition he was one of the
atoms!

He continued to walk onward to Columbus Circle
and then out Central Park West. At his right, the
park, with its trees and rocks and playgrounds, its
bridle paths, its young women in riding breeches accompanied by riding masters. Apartment houses
reared above him. New edifices arising. Laborers
upon the new Subway warning pedestrians of an im-
minent blast. Women with stereotyped faces leading little dogs. Uniformed doormen. . . . Still New
York—still New York in character, and unmistak-
able!

At Eighty-fifth Street he turned to the left and
presently entered one of the more modest apartment
houses—a walk-up. He was an hour late; but even
now he did not hurry, was strangely reluctant to
mount those flights of stairs to his home. And now
his face wore again that expression of uneasiness, of
perplexity, of perturbation, which it had worn as
he came from his office.

He opened the door with his latchkey and closed
it after him softly, almost as if he did not wish to
be heard entering. But he was heard, for Janet
called a trifle sharply, "Is that you, Ren?"

"Yes," he said.

She came into the hall to kiss him. "Well," she
said, "you're an hour late! Subway break down?"

"I walked up," he said.

"Walked up! The idea!—and me waiting luncheon for you!"

"I forgot luncheon," he said.

That was so unlike him—to forget luncheon or to forget anything else—that Janet felt a little twinge of alarm. "You're not sick?" she asked.

"No. I just walked up. I wanted to think."

"Something," said Janet, "has happened."

By this time they were in the living room, and Warren dropped into a chair. He dreaded telling his wife; was suddenly conscious there was a great deal about her that he did not know; that he knew but one phase of her and had seen her in but one environment. He temporized.

"I'm raised a hundred a month," he said.

"A hundred a month!" Her active mind commenced at once to play with this addition to their resources. "That's nothing to be glum about."

"And a house. I understand it's a practically new house, and modern and all that."

Janet's brows puckered. "A house!"

"Yes, and the use of a car."

She got up and came to stand by the arm of his chair. "Would you mind starting at the beginning?" she asked. "What house and what car—and what's the idea?"

"Mr. Dinsmore called me in this morning. He told me what I knew already—that the Colchester mill isn't getting the results it should. He said I seemed to be able to straighten out muddles. And then he said they wanted me to go up there and take hold, and that they'd give me a hundred more a month, and this house to live in and the company car."

"You mean—you don't mean we'd have to go and live in that place?"

"Colchester? Yes, we'd have to live there."

"And leave New York?" Warren said nothing. "I won't do it! I won't! I won't be dragged off to live in some hole. . . . You don't have to go, do you?"

"I don't have to. I've until Monday to make up my mind."

"Well, you don't need until Monday," Janet said with decision. "You tell them they can just keep their old hundred-dollar raise, and we'll stay right where we are."

"I was afraid you'd feel that way," Warren said, "but let's think it over and talk it over. Let's hear what Sarah has to say. You know, Janet, I don't want to go away to the wilderness any more than you do, but ——"

"But what?"

"Well, you know how it is with a big concern like the Consolidated. It's hard to get ahead, and slow. Now they seem to have taken notice of me ——"

"But," interrupted Janet, "they wouldn't discharge you if you told them you wouldn't go."

"No," Warren said hesitatingly, "but they'd sort

of lose interest in me. I'd be forgotten. Business is pretty arbitrary. If it offers you a chance and you turn it down, you're not likely to be offered another. . . . No, it would mean looking for another job eventually, unless we could be contented to have me stay where I am forever."

"Maybe even that would be better than dragging off to some terrible place. . . . What sort of town is this Colchester, and where is it?"

"It's in Vermont. The population is something like twelve hundred." Here Warren put Colchester's best foot forward. "The mills are down the river about three miles. Mr. Dinsmore says it's a fine little place."

"He would. He doesn't have to live there. No theaters, I suppose, and maybe no movie. Heavens! And we'd leave all our friends behind! Ren, what in the world would we do for people to talk to? What kind of people live in those towns?"

"I'm afraid I don't know any more about it than you, dear. Pretty dreadful, I guess."

"And how long would we have to stay—forever?"

"Oh, not forever. Mr. Dinsmore said a couple of years or so; just until I can get things straightened out."

"And what about Sarah? I suppose you and I could exist, but what about her? And just at this age too! What sort of young men would she meet? What would there be for her to do? She'd die!"

"I was thinking about Sarah," Warren said

slowly. "It'll be pretty hard on her, and we've got to think about her. She's twenty, and in a couple of years she ought to be marrying."

"A fine chance in your Colchester!" said Janet witheringly.

"It's a hard place to put a man," Warren said in the voice of one who is harried by events almost past his endurance. "I know what I ought to decide. I know what it means. I know what it means to turn this thing down, but I can't bear to go for the sake of you girls, and for my own sake."

"Two years!" Janet said despairingly. Then: "If we do take it I refuse to go native, as the books say about the South Sea Islands. I shan't do that! I'll—I'll keep up. I'll not allow myself to degenerate into one of those people. The Lord knows I'll have time enough for reading and music and things!"

"Anyhow we could save money," Warren said dejectedly. "In two years, with what we have, we could get together enough to buy a mighty nice apartment."

"In two years," said Janet, "we wouldn't remember how to behave in an apartment."

Warren lay back in his chair and pressed his thumbs against his eyes; Janet recognized the symptom and frowned. "Forget it now," she said, "or you'll be working yourself up to one of those nervous headaches. It isn't too late to run around to the movies. That'll take our minds off it for a while."

"Where's Sarah?"

"Gadding," Janet said succinctly. "Come along."

They went downstairs and crossed over to Broadway. It was pretty remote from Forty-second Street, but it was still Broadway. On another block or so was Riverside Drive, where reared those so-desirable apartments which they coveted; those buildings where one could buy in fee simple a section of the fourth floor or of the tenth floor, involving a common ownership of the elevators and the heating plant and the uniformed attendant at the door, and the canvas porte-cochère to be erected on stormy days. There was nothing bizarre in this to the Cross family—nothing abnormal about buying a home which did not touch a foot of earth, or about owning a dwelling surrounded top, bottom and both sides by other dwellings like a cell in a honeycomb. In them had never been born that passion, once common to mankind, for ownership of the soil. Soil was something that parks were made of.

It was not unnatural to them to have no neighbors; to dwell for years in a building with a half dozen or a dozen other tenants and not even to know them by name; to have no acquaintance within the radius of half a dozen blocks. This was life as they knew it, life as they understood it, life as they always had lived it; and they saw nothing wrong with it. Perhaps there was nothing wrong with it. Every civilization builds according to its necessities; every society organizes according to what it breeds within itself and to guard itself from what it has itsel

created. The more complex any body of society, the more complex and efficient must be the protective machinery of each individual in it. And New York has been artful in devising expedients.

Janet felt something of that sensation which had impelled her husband to walk home from the office. She touched his arm. "Let's not see the picture," she said. "Let's go over to the Drive and walk."

He nodded acquiescence, and waiting their opportunity, they scurried through a gap in the traffic and reached the other shore; then onward to the Drive and the river.

"What more can anybody want than this?" Janet said to herself; but her eyes and her thoughts were not on the majesty of the great river or on the splendor of the cliffs which lifted themselves upon the opposite shore. They were not upon the romance of the transactions taking place upon that water within range of her eyes; not upon the dingy tramp steamers anchored now after sailing distant seas and touching at strange ports; not upon bristling little ferryboats, battling the current and squawling their demands to tugs and barges and scows; not upon the great masses of canal boats, bearing from the north lumber and bricks and the Lord knew what to supply the demands of a mammoth aggregation of ever-demanding human beings. No, her thoughts were upon those gorgeous piles of brick and stone and steel which fronted on the avenue; elegant hornets' nests inhabited by the fortunate of the earth who had

achieved their hearts' desire; by rich men and women, by singularly fortunate children who might play in the park below under the hired eyes of Scandinavian or Italian or French or English nursemaids; by exotic dogs, and actors and merchants and old ladies with a competence and abdomens.

They walked in silence, Warren and Janet, but their minds were alike occupied with the dread of leaving all this, of giving up these marvels, these supreme advantages of comfort and culture and civilization for something unknown but necessarily lacking in all these essentials. They reflected upon the harshness of life which could have the heartlessness to demand of them such a sacrifice.

Warren knew, in spite of what he said or implied to his wife, that he must go. He knew it would be impossible to decline this opportunity which came wearing so unpleasant a face. And Janet knew it too. She would fight against it, pretend she would not go, but she would go. Basically she was sound. Until the decision must be made she derived a bitter pleasure from pretending.

They turned back at Grant's Tomb, crossing the street to walk beside the stone wall which guarded the descent to the river. They walked slowly, mournfully, in a sort of funeral march, a farewell processional. When they reached their street again they turned in silence, and, still silently, they reached their home. Not until they were again in the living room did either of them speak, but then Warren said apathetically, "Gosh, I hate to tell Sarah!"

Janet's eyes snapped; then she shrugged her shoulders. "You can never tell about Sarah. She raises the most frightful rows when you can see no reason for them, and behaves like a lambkin when you expect her to throw a fit. But she'll have to take her medicine like the rest of us."

It will be seen the decision had been reached. The Cross family was to transplant itself from the soil in which it had flourished, and was to adventure, like some transplanted, exotic, flowering shrub into a new climate and a different garden where it must adapt itself or perish.

Presently Sarah came in, buoyant, excited as always, dark, keen, flashing, and hurled her bit of a hat upon the davenport.

"Rotten show," she said. "Rotten music, and that man is a washout."

"Sit down and draw a breath," said Warren. He cleared his throat. "How'd you like to leave New York?"

Sarah turned from the mirror with a quick, pert, birdlike motion of her head. "You know the answer to that one," she said. "Think up another that's louder and funnier."

"To a town up in Vermont where we'd live in a house and have a car?"

"And do what with both of them?" Sarah asked. "Grow pumpkins?"

"You might as well get used to the idea," Janet said a trifle belligerently. "On the first of the month we move to Colchester bag and baggage—and that's that."

Sarah stared a moment, made a little grimace with nose and mouth, and turned her head from one to the other. "Well, I'll be darned!" she said almost casually. "I'm going to hate it!"

With that she went out of the room toward her own chamber, leaving Warren and his wife in a state of relief and amazement.

Warren waggled his head. "She's a notch beyond me," he said.

"Anyhow we can give thanks she didn't kick and scream," said Janet.

"But I'm sorry for the kid. It'll be worse on her than on us."

"It can't be," Janet said emphatically.

CHAPTER II

NOTHING could be seen through the rain and the mist save the dingy, faded front of the station and a few drunken lumber piles off at the right. It was dark and cold. The journey from New York, with its changes of trains and waits, had been irritatingly irksome, and no member of the Cross family was in cheerful humor. Warren helped down his wife and sister to the soggy platform, and there they stood shivering.

"Heavens!" exclaimed Janet, shoulders drawn together and teeth chattering.

She had made up her mind to hate Colchester, and somehow it lifted her spirits to find it worse than her imaginings. She noted with satisfaction that her husband wore a harried, bewildered look, and did not appear to know what to do next. Wives have a way of deriving satisfaction from their husbands' moments of incompetency. "Well," she asked, "aren't we going to do something? Are we going to stand here in the rain all night?"

"It's a nice fresh country rain," said Sarah—this irony referring back to certain attempts on the part of her brother to paint encouraging pictures of their future home.

"There must be a cab or something," Warren said,

and turning to a fat man in overalls asked, "How do we get to the hotel?"

"Bus'll be here in a minute, I guess. Suthin' must 'a' kept him," was the answer.

Then a flivver splashed up dismally to the platform, and a second fat man appeared, wearing a rubber raincoat and boots and a sou'wester. He was rather more than fat—he was chubby, and his wet cheeks gleamed red as he passed a lighted window. Evidently a healthy person.

"Folks goin' to the hotel," said the first fat man.

"Git in then," said the second fat man, eying them amiably. "Kind of wet, hain't it? Got any baggage checks? Git in and I'll be with you in a minute."

They got into the car and shrank from the clammy wet surface of the leather upholstery.

"I thought they always had reception committees and bands in these towns to meet arriving notables," said Sarah.

Presently their driver returned, taking ample time to settle himself comfortably. "Hain't Mr. Cross, be ye?" he asked. "Got a letter from him reservin' rooms."

"I'm Mr. Cross," said Warren, without warmth.

"Pleased to meet ye," said the fat man, extending a soggy hand. Sarah giggled.

They splashed away into the wet darkness, turned acutely, the tires making a distressing, soughing sound in the mud, and commenced the descent of a hill. Nothing was visible save yellow lights now and

then, muffled by the rain. No one seemed to be
abroad. They crossed a tiny bridge and proceeded
for a few hundred yards along the level, and then,
turning to the left, crossed another bridge. Store
fronts were to be seen dimly on either hand, and the
black, impending bulk of maples. With a jerk they
turned into a driveway and stopped beneath a porte-
cochère.

"Here we be," said the driver. "Go right in. I'll
fetch your luggage."

They walked, shivering, along a broad veranda
fronted by white columns and entered a spacious
doorway, to come face to face with a broad fireplace
in which burned amiably a great log upon its carefully preserved bed of ashes. Over the fireplace
were a pair of flintlocks crossed over a huge pewter
tray, and rush-bottomed armchairs were grouped in
a half circle, occupied by men who became silent
suddenly and eyed the newcomers furtively. Janet
and Sarah scrutinized these men as furtively as they
themselves were being appraised, and found not a
tailored suit among them. One man, who had been
wearing a straw hat, removed it and arose.

"Maybe the ladies 'ud like to get up by the fire,"
he said.

"Thank you," Warren said shortly. He was embarrassed, ill at ease, conscious of the scrutiny, and
wholly without knowledge of how to conduct himself
in this emergency, or to estimate the place and quality of these loungers. However, the driver, who

turned out to be also the proprietor of the hotel, saved him prolonged annoyance by appearing breezily.

"Cal'late you want to go to your rooms," he said. "I'll show ye up. Tend to registerin' later. This way."

He led them through a door and up carpeted stairs to the second floor, then along a corridor to a selected door, which he opened.

"Adjoinin' rooms, with bath between," he said amiably. "Anythin' else?"

"Nothing, thank you," said Warren, and reached into his pocket. "When can we have dinner?"

"Supper's ready in ten minutes," said the fat man, eying with some amazement the fifty cents Warren extended to him, comprehended its meaning finally and grinned to exhibit a broken front tooth. "What's that fer? Seems like we don't do much tippin' up this way."

It wasn't a rebuke; it was not ungracious; it was simply the statement of a fact; but Warren blushed furiously as if he had been caught in some outrageous gaucherie.

"Come down to the dinin' room whenever you git ready," said the fat man; and out he waddled, stepping wide and betraying a great wrinkle across the back of his ill-fitting coat. The door closed upon him.

"It's clean!" exclaimed Janet, who had been allowing her eyes to dart about the room.

"I'm going to catch him and exhibit him," Sarah said pertly.

"Catch whom?"

"The fat one who wouldn't take a tip. I thought it was against the law to refuse tips."

"And there's a regular bathroom," Janet said. "It's all neat, anyhow," she said grudgingly. "You run along and change, Sarah. I'm hungry."

"Funny nobody from the mill came to meet me," Warren said aggrievedly. He frowned. "They knew I was coming tonight."

Twenty minutes later they went down to supper in the bare but meticulously clean, almost blatantly neat, dining-room. There was no menu card, but a nice-looking girl in white recited to them the dishes of the evening. The food was plain but excellent; the biscuits were noteworthy, and it was their first experience of being served with maple sirup as a dessert—little sauce dishes filled with what they never would have recognized as maple sirup from its color. It was not of a reddish shade, as was all the sirup they ever had encountered, but was more the tint of champagne.

Weary as they were, and inclined to be despondent, there was no conversation. Finished with their maple sirup, they pushed back their chairs and returned to their rooms.

"Warren," said Janet, "if you'll open these trunks and then clear out, I'll pack away our things."

"Can't I help?" he asked, without enthusiasm. Janet sniffed.

Warren descended again, but a glance told him the rain was still falling dismally, so he returned and dropped into a chair before the fireplace. He was alone. The others who had occupied those chairs were still at their supper. He lighted a cigarette and sat back to enjoy the blaze and his own heavy thoughts. . . . Rain! There would be many rainy nights, and what would they do with them? In New York one could step into the Subway and reach a theater——

Presently three men issued from the dining-room, one of them picking his teeth leisurely and appearing to derive deep satisfaction from it. They selected chairs, sat down with sidewise glances at Warren and lighted cigars. After a time the man with the toothpick spoke.

"All wrong, Jim," he said. "They ought to be made to pay every cent, and regular interest too. They owe it, don't they? Borrowed it, didn't they? Well?"

"It was everybody's war," replied the man addressed as Jim. "We didn't get in to help at the start, and we didn't have such a sight of men killed, nor the sufferin' they did. Seems like the least we could do is forget them foreign debts."

A new figure had come in from outside—a young man, tall, angular, with lean face, gray eyes, rather pronounced cheek bones, faded reddish hair and lips which appeared to be locked shut by some unfailing device in his prominent chin. Warren glanced at him carelessly, then studied his face with interest. It commanded his attention, though it was not the face of a gentleman as that term is understood in the neighborhood of Wall Street. It was not a carefully tended face, though smoothly shaven. Its owner appeared to have been careless about leaving it out in the weather. About his clothing he seemed to have been equally thoughtless; what he wore evidently had been purchased with the sole thought of covering his person, and not at all for its embellishment. His hands were large and his feet were large. But there was something about him which marked him as an individual.

He leaned over the back of a rocker listening until the man named Jim had finished, then he uttered a dry cough, a sort of clearing of the throat preparatory to bringing into action the little-used machinery of his voice. "Own any Liberty Bonds?" he asked.

"Yes."

"Hope to be paid back what they cost you?"

"You bet!"

"Who pays 'em back?"

"The Government to Washington."

"Where does it get the money to pay back?"

Jim thought a moment. "Taxes, I guess."

"Pay any?"

"A durn sight more'n I like."

"Where'd the Government get the money it loaned to these foreign countries?"

"I dunno. Taxes, maybe."

"Liberty Bonds," said the young man. "About a third of every Liberty Bond you own was loaned abroad."

"Huh!" said Jim doubtfully, waiting for the next development.

"Feel like accepting two-thirds of the face value of your bonds and letting it go at that?"

"Not by a jugful!"

"Feel like paying a third more taxes and giving it to France and Italy and the rest?"

"Not by a darn sight!"

"That," said the young man, "is what canceling the foreign debt means."

Warren continued to scrutinize this young user of the Socratic method of developing an argument. He was surprised. He was more than surprised, for even he himself, accustomed to finance as he was, had never thought of the matter in the light in which this young man presented it. Here was clear, concise thought, the swift checkmating of an opponent in argument. He was even mildly surprised at the subject matter of the argument; that men in this distant village so far from financial centers should be interested in such matters. He did not know that it was in such places as this, by such voices as these, that public opinion for the country is created; that it is so that men are lifted to eminence and parties carried forward to victory; that it is such little gatherings as this, in such little places as this, that rule the United States of America. He was sitting at the fountainhead of republican government and did not know it.

Presently Warren arose, feeling very awkward and out of place, but giving an impression of aloofness and offishness which he did not attend, and walked toward the stairs. Silence fell as several groups of eyes followed him.

"It's him," said the man called Jim as Warren passed out of earshot.

"Kind of uppish."

"Looks like he set store by himself."

The young man of the Socratic method pried open his lips again after that preparatory clearing of the throat. "I didn't notice anybody making him feel to home," he said; and without waiting to note the effect of his words, turned and walked out into the rain.

Warren opened the door to find his wife sitting on the floor surrounded by piles of clothing from their trunks. She was crying; down her cheeks ran silent tears which she was at no trouble to wipe away.

"Oh, Ren," she said, "it's so darn still! If only a taxi horn would squawk or an elevated train go by! It's—it's worse than I thought."

He agreed with her; the quiet appalled him, made him feel so remote, so strange. He had a feeling of being exiled, imprisoned, and a dreadful sensation

of impending monotony. What would there be to
do? He looked down at Janet helplessly. How
could he comfort her? Her weeping increased his
apprehensions. In addition to all he saw and con-
jectured and feared, was Janet going to go on like
this? Imagine coming home to a wife who was always crying with homesickness or the monotony of it!

"Listen, Janet――" he commenced, and something in his tone touched the hair trigger of the nervous tension under which she suffered.

"Oh, shut up!" she said; and then, burying her
face in the clean, cool, white counterpane, she burst
into a storm of sobbing.

Janet had behaved like this only once or twice
during the years of their married life, and it frightened and bewildered him now as it had done before.
And being frightened and bewildered he became
angry—angry and desperate. He knew that dreadful feeling of helplessness which all husbands come
to know; he felt that he was being treated unfairly,
and he wanted to argue about it. He wanted her to
stop and to admit that she was treating him unfairly
and to be sorry for it. Probably a million husbands
have known this same wish in comparable circumstances, but never a one has seen it fulfilled. Here
was a splendid commencement of a bitter night, which
neither of them desired, but which both seemed to
head for, urged by some irresistible contrariness.

Suddenly Sarah appeared in the bathroom door—
in a negligee which might have caused Colchester's

eyes to pop from its head. She wrinkled her nose at the spectacle.

"Shush!" she said peremptorily. "Lay off the family repartee! Ren, you boob, can't you see she's so tired she's on the verge of a conniption? Clear out while I put her to bed."

"I don't see you throwing any fits," Warren said untactfully.

She looked at him cornerwise. "Maybe," she said, "you think this promised land you've led us to doesn't make me feel like it."

Not being wholly bereft of reason he left the room and descended the stairs again. None was in the office but the chubby proprietor, who looked up amiably from his chair behind the desk.

"We don't have weather like this all the time," he said, with a grin which displayed that remaining half of a front tooth. "Sometimes it's worse."

Warren smiled wryly. "Have you any idea how long it will take for our furniture to get here?" he asked.

"No idee."

"By the way, who was the young man who came in while I sat here before—the one who squelched the argument about our foreign debts?"

"Name of Knuckles," said the proprietor, and bent over his books with an air of closing the audience.

CHAPTER III

JANET awoke first in the morning and got softly out of bed. A singularly brilliant sunlight, such sunlight as could only follow a downpour, and which owed something of its brilliance to the freshness of leaf and grass after the prolonged draught, made the outside world vibrate. She went to the window, and the life and richness of the air—the cool, tingling, early morning air—caressed her and stirred her hair. She breathed deeply and felt a trifle affronted to discover that she felt very well indeed, and very far from the tears of weariness and homesickness she had shed the night before.

Across from the hotel she saw a row of great maples, thick of bole, gigantic, shapely, gleaming green. Above and far beyond rose graciously the slope of the mountain, beautiful, restful; and the voice of the river reached her ears. To right and to left were houses gleaming white, so white and clean it seemed as if the painters must but that moment have taken down their ladders. Yet no paintbrush had touched their siding for years. Farther along was the livery barn, also white and clean, and beyond that the road meandered between low-set white houses on one side and white houses upon a little elevation, up which climbed little flights of steps, on the other side.

She saw no evidences of commerce or industry until she indiscreetly bent over the window sill and looked off to the right. There was a bridge of red ironwork and across it a sort of square upon the four corners of which rested stores. She knew them to be stores, though they were of wood and white as the dwelling houses. One especially well-kept building of two stories was the bank. She imagined correctly that other stores were upon the cross street, but somehow the locality had not the look of a business center. As far as she could see, there was no structure of brick, and no building which did not seem to rejoice in a fresh coat of white.

She turned from the window to find Warren sitting up in bed and rubbing his eyes. He always awakened slowly and found difficulty collecting his wits; now he muttered something unintelligible and ran his fingers through his hair. Then, as if some alarm had sounded, he hurled back the bedclothes and stood in the middle of the floor, blinking.

"It's a lovely morning, Ren," she said. "Come and look out."

He went with docility to the window and the fresh air played about his forehead and his eyes, sweeping away the fumes of profound sleep. He shook his head and blinked again.

"Gosh," he said, "but I slept! I don't remember going to bed."

"I'm sorry I made such an idiot of myself last night," Janet said. "But I was worn out and nervous—and that horrid rain. I'm going to make the best of it—honestly I am."

Warren patted her shoulder. "Sure," he said. "We all are. . . . What time is it?"

She looked at her little traveling clock. It was 7:30. "It's so still," she said apprehensively. "Do you suppose it is always so still?"

"I wonder when they have breakfast. . . . Is Sarah up?"

She went to see while Warren made his toilet and got into his clothes. He was thinking about the mill now—how he would get there—if any of these Perrigo men would call at the hotel for him. He wondered what they looked like and what the mills looked like and what sort of office he would find. Perrigo! He visualized these former owners of the mill, who had continued to operate it after it had been purchased by the Consolidated—Walter, who ran the mill end; and James, who ran the woods end—and he hoped they would not see fit to make things difficult for him. But he was worried. Men resent being supplanted; and even though he had been directed to retain them in their places if it should be feasible to do so, he would nevertheless have to assume a position of authority over them in a business to which they had been born and in which they had been raised.

He went downstairs while Janet dressed. There was no one in the office and the dining-room was closed. On the piazza, a row of big rush-bottomed rockers were tilted, heels in the air and faces downward against the wall, and he swung one of these around and sat down. . . . Colchester! He was here, and New York was way back there somewhere! He made a futile effort to appraise Colchester. There was nothing to appraise. So far as he could see there was nothing but trees and white houses and forest-clad mountain. He did not know what to make of it.

So far he had not seen a living soul, but presently a man in a straw hat and shirt sleeves came along and rolled back the door of the livery stable and garage; then a group of Italian laborers passed with lunch boxes, and a thin old man splashed past in a buggy. It looked as if nothing ever happened there, and as if nothing would ever happen. But he could not deny that it was rather pleasing, what he could see of it, and that view of the distant mountain through the clear vibrant air was unquestionably beautiful.

A Standard Oil wagon clattered past with a young man in a blue flannel shirt upon the seat, and a rooster crowed. Then he was conscious of a musical cheeping of birds. A tall stooping man came and stood in the door of the grocery across the way, and another man, leaning over the railing of the bridge, called a greeting. "Mornin', Henry."

"Mornin', Pazzy."

"River come up some in the night."

"Not to hurt."

"Spile the fishin' for a week."

"Seems as though," said the grocer, and disappeared into his store.

These, thought Warren, were some of his future townsmen, among whom he was to live. Not that he thought to know them, for in New York one did not know his grocer socially. He wondered whom he would know socially. Not the collarless man on the bridge who seemed exercised about the fishing, certainly!

By the time Janet and Sarah came out to him he had seen a dozen people, including a couple of barefoot boys. And here was the center of town. He contrasted it with the morning rush hour in the Subway.

"So this," said Sarah, looking about her, "is Paris!" She lifted her shoulders. "I feel like the beneficiary of a fresh-air fund. Is this the sort of place they send them to?"

"Probably," Warren said absently.

"Heavens, look at the traffic jam!" Sarah exclaimed, for two horse-drawn vehicles and a motor car appeared simultaneously upon the square.

"The dining-room door's open," Janet said.

They breakfasted—and not without cheerfulness. It is not easy to be disconsolate on such a morning; and even so far from Broadway, it is difficult to be weighed down with boredom at eight o'clock. When they were finished Warren stepped to the desk.

"Anyone asking for me?" he inquired.

"Not yit."

"How do I reach the mills?"

"Perrigo Mills?"

"Yes."

"Wa-al, you can walk. Follow the river a mite more'n three mile. Kind of muddy though. Or Smith'll drive you down—across the street yonder."

He found his wife and sister in rockers on the piazza. "I suppose I ought to get in touch with things this morning," he said. "I'll not be gone all day. Think you can find something to do?"

"We'll explore," said Janet.

He frowned. "It's queer nobody comes around," he said. "They knew I was coming last night."

"If we get lost," Sarah said, "we'll inquire our way of a policeman."

"I'll try to get back by noon," Warren said, and they watched him cross the road to the livery, where, having negotiated with its proprietor, he presently entered an automobile and was driven away.

Janet and Sarah sat for fifteen minutes, and then by common consent arose and walked down the street to the square, past the bank with its plate-glass windows, and glanced up a stairway going up in its rear upon whose treads were cardboard signs giving the information that John Watts was a Notary Public and Fire Insurance; that Thomas Hewitt was an Attorney at Law and that Titus Lowrie was a Doctor of Dental Surgery. Next came a hardware store, which seemed also to sell canned provisions; and a tinsmith, and a barber shop which projected out over the river. Inside they could see a pool table and two chairs and two large cabinets filled with individual shaving mugs.

That was the end of things on that side of the street, for it became river bank; and they paused for a time to watch the swirling, foamy, yellowish water as it rushed by in flood. Beyond they could see the hill climbing upward, and more white houses loftily perched. Opposite was the public library back of its well-kept lawn and its stereotyped monument of a sailor in the uniform and forage cap of '65 leaning on his musket. It was a pleasant, homelike little building, the only structure of brick in the village of Colchester. They crossed and passed more stores, some with wooden awnings, some with piazzas which one had to mount in order to enter, which had a sort of jumbled look within. Window dressing had made scant progress in Colchester, though the haberdashery made some pretense of it. They took note of drug stores which also sold wall paper and groceries and ten-penny nails and farm implements, and of a couple of fruit stores run by Italians—something more than a dozen stores.

"Heavens!" said Janet.

"What price window shopping?" Sarah inquired, with a shrug.

"I wonder where our house is?"

"No idea. Is anything wrong with either of us? Skirt hanging or anything?"

"Why?"

"Everybody we pass turns to stare."

"Maybe it's a custom of the country."

"It's certainly a custom of the country to go without coats."

"I haven't seen anybody who is our kind yet."

"Did Ren know when the furniture would be here?"

"He guessed ten days or two weeks."

"Then let's go back to the hotel till I unpack. I can't live out of a trunk as long as that."

It was something more than an hour later when they came downstairs and again took seats on the piazza. There were more people on the streets now; the village wore quite an air of life, but most of the people to be seen were men.

"Do they allow women here?" Sarah asked.

"I suppose," Janet rejoined, "they're all at home now doing the washing or something. I wonder what these women can do. What's that building next door?"

"No idea. . . . Here's one of them now. See?— coming this way in a blue runabout. Um-m-m." This was a sort of appraising hum.

The little car stopped before the hotel, and a girl thrust open the door and sprang out. One uses the word "sprang" advisedly. Then she ran up the walk and fairly leaped up the steps. So swiftly did she arrive that there was scant time for observation, yet Janet and Sarah noted that she wore her gloriously auburn hair in a modish bob and that it curled deliciously. They noted her shoes, as women will, and saw that they came from the right sort of shop; they took stock of slender shapely legs in silk stockings, of a skirt and sweater which indicated not only good taste and an appreciation for the right colors but a certain purchasing power in dollars and cents. This was all they had time to catalogue in the few seconds before the girl stood upon the piazza.

She halted with her hand outstretched to open the screen, looked at Janet and Sarah with a little frown of uncertainty, and then advanced toward them. They saw now that her face was patrician. That was one's first impression. A reader of physiognomy might have gone further and seen in it willfulness, daring to recklessness, hunger for life and a keen intelligence. Given time for study he might have seen a certain wistfulness and lines of humor about the eyes. Anyone could see the exquisite complexion and, as she spoke, a possession of white, flawless, beautiful teeth.

"Is this Mrs. Cross?" she asked.

"I am Mrs. Cross."

"I'm Eunice Perrigo." She pronounced the name as if it were all-explanatory, as, indeed, it would have been to anyone familiar with Colchester and its history. "Walter didn't stop on the way to the mill, did he? I knew he wouldn't, so somebody in the family's got to show a trace of decent manners.

James might have come if I'd told him to, but he's back in the camps."

"I don't understand," said Janet. "Who are James and Walter?"

"My brothers. And, of course, they don't like it—especially Walter. But I told him it served him right. He had no business selling the mill, and there was a fine row about it. But he talked James into it, and he's my guardian for another year yet, so what could I do?"

"Oh," said Janet, "I think I understand. It was your family who owned the mill Mr. Cross has come to take charge of."

"Grandpa started it and father built it up—and the boys sold it. And now they've no kick coming. We Perrigos don't agree—always. You'll learn that soon enough in this town. So I ran down as soon as I could to give you the keys of the city and all that."

"Awfully sweet of you," said the somewhat nonplused Janet. "This is Mr. Cross' sister, Miss Perrigo."

Eunice Perrigo extended her hand with a boyish gesture and bobbed her head in a manner both brisk and decisive. "I'm glad you're here—whatever Walter thinks about it. I like new people. I like lots of people. Do you play tennis and things?"

"I'm afraid not," Sarah said; "but I suppose I can learn."

"Of course. I'll teach you. We've a good court

at the house. You're going to live in the mill house, aren't you? There's a court there too. Have you seen it? Lovely view and I'm sure you'll like it. Suppose we get in the car and drive up that way. We can squeeze in."

"Of course we're curious to see where we're going to live," said Janet.

"Come along then. We'll see all the sights before dinner. . . . There's a dance tonight." Her mind seemed to flash from subject to subject, following no definite order; she seemed hurried, breathless, feverishly eager.

They crowded into the little car and whisked away. "I haven't a megaphone," Eunice said; "but outside that, this is as good a sight-seeing car as any."

"Oh!" exclaimed Janet, and felt suddenly lonesome. "Oh, I could kiss a Chinatown bus! I could hug a Subway guard!"

"Do you live here all the time?" Sarah asked.

"Twelve months out of twelve, since I finished school."

"How do you ———" Sarah was going to ask how she could stand it, but arrested that question in mid-career. "What do you do? What is there to do? Are there nice people here?"

"Come to the dance tonight," Eunice said. "You'll see us all—all that are able to walk."

"Where is it?"

"Memorial Hall—next to the hotel."

"A public dance?"

Eunice nodded. "Dollar a couple, including ice cream and cake."

"But—but do people go to public dances? I mean the sort of people you want to meet?"

"Do they go to cabarets and supper clubs in New York?" Eunice countered with good-humored malice. "Oh, yes, we all go—and sometimes bring the babies."

"Does—does one dress?"

"Women wear what they like. But if you mean men, Mrs. Cross, a man who showed up wearing evening dress would be mistaken for a Swiss Bell Ringer and asked to perform. The only time we see dress suits is when the Chautauqua course is on—and on the screen."

"Oh, you do have movies then?"

"Tuesday, Thursday and Saturday. . . . Darn him!" Suddenly she jammed on her brakes and brought the car to a skidding stop, a measure necessary to avoid running down a young man who, apparently deep in thought, with bent head, stepped off the sidewalk into the road. Her cheeks were an angry red as she leaned over the wheel.

"Why don't you watch where you're going?" she demanded.

The young man, apparently not startled, lifted his thin angular face and regarded her with gray eyes in which there was no light of amusement, but rather a cold, detached stare which seemed hardly to see her at all.

"Good morning, Eunice," he said, but without lifting his hat; and then walked on deliberately, head dropped again, for all the world as if he had not been interrupted in his crossing at all.

Janet raised her eyebrows as well-bred ladies sometimes do when the event is not to their taste. "How odd!" she said.

Eunice sent the car forward with a jerk, her cheeks still flaming. "Oh," she said presently, "I despise that man!"

"Who is he?"

It seemed for a moment that Eunice would not reply, but then she said with an edged voice, "Knuckles is his name."

"Knuckles! Actually? Is that a name?"

"You'll find it is when you've lived here long enough. It's a name, and Perrigo is a name, and the two don't eat out of the same dish. But it's not on account of that I despise him; it's on his own account. I don't care what Walter thinks or what James thinks. I can do my own liking or disliking. It makes no difference to me that his father and mine hated each other. I just can't bear him. There's something about him sets my teeth on edge and always has."

"M-m-m!" said Janet diplomatically. "What does he do?"

"Do? Nothing. He dickers."

"Dickers? I don't think I understand."

"He buys and sells things—anything from a pig to a sawmill. 'Dickers' is the only word for it."

"How odd!" Janet said for the second time.

But Eunice was talking again. It seemed to Janet and Sarah that she was singularly frank in her disclosures of her family's affairs. "I don't know what the original row was about—between my father and Squire Knuckles. Probably money. It happened when Walter's mother was alive. Walter and I are only half brother and sister. All three of us are only half—father was married three times. Probably that's why we get along like cats and dogs. . . . We turn at the next road," she said, dropping the subject of the Knuckles-Perrigo feud with characteristic suddenness. "Your house is about a mile down. You get a view down the valley and right across to Colchester Mountain. Wait till you see."

They drove on until presently they saw before them a large white house which, in spite of its newness, seemed to be a part of the old town. It was an excellent house in the Colonial manner, roomy and satisfying. Lonely it might be, for there were no neighboring houses, and its back fence was encroached upon by the underbrush of the woods. Below it the hill dropped rapidly to the river; and beyond was the thread of road, a scattering of houses and barns and fields; then, impending over all, the great mountain, massive, green, gracious. The forests with which it was covered seemed no taller than blades of grass, now green where grew beech

and birch and maple, now black where the spruces
thrust upward their pyramids to the sky. And across
its sunny face moved cloud shadows.

"It's lovely," Janet exclaimed; "but"—turning
to survey the house and its surroundings—"so
lonely!" She smiled apologetically. "We've always
lived in an apartment, you know. People above and
below and on both sides. It—I hope I shall get used
to it."

"There are the mills," Eunice said, pointing to the
south where smoke arose from a great stack, and
where low buildings rambled and piles of lumber
clustered. There was a stretch of placid mill pond,
a footbridge across the dam; and then the valley shut
in, hill shouldering hill. "I used to love them when
I was little. All day long I've ridden the saw carriage, and I could dog as well as any of the crew.
They never let me saw!" She said this as if it were
a very real deprivation. "But I never go there now.
I've never set foot there since Walter sold. . . .
Want to look in the windows? Maybe we can find
one unlocked."

But none was unfastened, so they must content
themselves with peering in as best they could; and
then, urged by Eunice, who seemed unable to rest in
any spot for more than a minute, they reëntered the
car and drove back into the village. Through the
town they whisked, and up another hill along a street
lined with large comfortable homes in broad yards,
each with its huge barn—few of which were now used

for their original purpose. Automobiles stood where once the matched span had clattered shod hoofs on splintered floor.

"There's my house," Eunice said, pointing to a long, low structure upon a hilltop. "Dad built it. Architects and everything. I'd like it if it wasn't so big. But it's mine—my own. It was left to me, and Walter knows what would happen if he tried to sell it. Want to come in? Glass of buttermilk or something?"

"Thank you, no. We'd better be getting back. Mr. Cross is coming up from the mills to luncheon. . . . And you've no idea how we appreciate your coming for us."

At the hotel they disembarked with further thanks, and Eunice and the blue runabout rushed away.

"Well!" exclaimed Janet. "And what do you think of her?"

"I liked her," Sarah said with customary directness.

"She took my breath away. And doesn't she talk! Do you suppose everybody here is so discoursive about their family affairs? But she is pretty. . . . I wonder what her brothers are like."

"We'll probably hear from Ren," said Sarah. "There goes a whistle. I suppose that means it's noon."

It was, completing their first morning in Colchester. They went to their rooms to make ready for the midday meal, and there awaited the arrival of Warren rather more eagerly than either had been accustomed to do. In New York his coming home from work had been simply a coming home; here, in these strange surroundings, it took on the dignity of an event.

CHAPTER IV

IT WAS after supper that Sarah brought up the question of the dance. "Let's go and know the worst," she said. "Miss Perrigo told us we'd see the whole menagerie."

"We don't know anybody," Warren objected. "I'd feel like a fool."

"Didn't you meet Walter and James then?" Janet asked.

"Walter and James? What're you talking about?"

"Perrigo," said Janet. "We've been hearing about them from their extraordinary sister—family skeletons and everything. I gather that sister and Walter don't agree. James remained rather indefinite."

"Oh, the Perrigos! I've been with Walter all day, but James kept out of range. I gather he's a queer egg. Sort of half Indian and the other half wildcat, if you follow me."

"We don't," said Sarah, "but you interest us. And that's a godsend—already."

"He's in charge of the woods end. They're his natural element, from all accounts. Sort of a will-o'-the-wisp johnny. Turns up at odd times and in odd places. They say he's apt to get up at one o'clock in the morning and start off cross lots through the woods for some lumber camp ten miles away—as likely to do that as to stay in bed. Knows the wild flowers and calls deer by their first names."

"Sounds thrilling. And his age?"

"I didn't ask. Younger than his brother by quite a lot, I got the idea."

"And what about Walter?—who, we were told, resented us very much."

Warren wrinkled his forehead and squinted one eye. "I'm not prepared to recite on Walter. He is all grays. Verges on middle age, verges on baldness, verges on stoutness. I couldn't make out whether he was doing a heap of thinking or none at all. I'm quite sure he resents my being sent here, but he didn't have any chip on his shoulder. He's no gay cavalier. Either he's a cipher or else what the English call a downy bird."

"Let's go to that dance," said Sarah.

"I'll tell you," Janet said, "let's go down and sit on the porch, and if the music sounds good we might just look in."

They did go down, to be met in the lower hall by Mrs. Knowles, wife of the proprietor of the hotel. They had seen her during the day, but had not encountered her directly. She came up to them smiling so friendly a smile that even these bred New Yorkers recognized the genuineness of it. A round, red-cheeked matron was Mrs. Knowles, who dressed her feet in large and comfortable shoes and did not

conform at any point to the modern ideal of the
feminine figure. But her voice was soft, and there
was that splendid old New England speech to lend
to her a certain distinction. All New Englanders of
the real stock possess this distinction when they
speak; it is eloquent of cleanly bred race, and in its
accents and stresses and archaic forms there is an
unconscious dignity.

"I'm sorry I haven't had time to speak to you
ladies before," she said; "but what with one movin'
in and another movin' out, and chambermaids what
they be, I haven't had a minute to myself all day.
'Twan't lack of friendliness, I want you should know
that."

"Of course," said Janet, rather amazed at her
sensations—first, that she did not find Mrs. Knowles
the laughable, crude, small-town character her appearance might have indicated, and second, that she
was able to sense no superiority of class in herself. It
was apparent Mrs. Knowles sensed no such possibility. "You must be very busy, indeed."

"We hope you'll like it while you're with us, my
husband and I. We want you should feel right to
home, and if there's anything we can do to make you
comfortable ——"

"I'm sure we're as comfortable as can be."

"Now that's nice. I know how 'tis movin' to a
new place. You feel strange and all. I know jest
how to feel for you. I was sayin' to my husband
today I must have some ladies in some afternoon this

week to meet you. Maybe a dozen or so, and we'll play bridge—them that cares to—and five hundred —and some refreshments. Now le' me see—Thursday? No, better say Friday."

"Why, Mrs. Knowles——" Janet did not know what to say. Was it correct to know socially the wife of the keeper of this little country inn, and to accept what she offered? To what would it bind her? Would she be making a false step in taking up with the wrong crowd?

Mrs. Knowles was incapable of comprehending such a doubt. "Now don't say a word. I love to do it. . . . Goin' in to the dance? Ab Knuckles gets over good music, I'll say that for him. 'Twan't so good before he started in."

"Mr. Knuckles? What has he to do with the dance?"

"He gives 'em. Rents Memorial Hall by the year, and runs the pictures and all. It seems like Knuckles kind of takes holt of anythin' nobody else seems to manage. . . . I see you ridin' with Eunice this mornin'. Sometimes my heart jest goes out to that girl. . . . Well, you'll be wantin' to go along now. . . . Mind you, my husband and I want to see you jest as comfortable as you can be."

"Thank you, Mrs. Knowles," Janet said, and, when the busy, bustling, kindly woman had hurried on to some unfinished task, she turned to her sister. "Well!" she exclaimed. "And what does one do about that? I—well, it's one way of doing, I suppose."

"I—if I were you, Janet, I wouldn't snub her," said Warren. "I'm sure she means well."

"But to have a party for me! I never heard of such a thing! What shall I do? And she seems a nice old thing too."

"I presume the grocer will be giving a ball for us if we go in there to buy a pound of butter," Sarah said laughingly, and feeling quite certain she had uttered a comical absurdity. "Oh, come on, let's see this performance. It must be respectable, anyhow, or Eunice Perrigo wouldn't be going. She may be a queer one, but she'd pass in any crowd."

They sat down on the piazza to give themselves a chance to make up their minds about it, and were really interested to see the crowd gathering. Young men and women walked up and down; unattached young men stood along the sidewalk, smoking and thinking of humorous things to say as people went past; two boys were doing a profitable business with a pop-corn wagon. There was much standing around outside the door of Memorial Hall by men whose women evidently had preceded them inside; and, what seemed strangest of all to these New Yorkers, everybody seemed to know everybody else. First names were used. Even young men, speaking to white-haired elders, used the familiar form of address in many instances, and with an air of custom which savored not at all of impertinence.

"I haven't seen a well-dressed woman yet," said Janet.

"I don't know," Warren said; "seems to me I've seen several rather decent-looking couples."

"Well," said Sarah, "if you see a young man who looks as if he knew his way around, tag him for me."

Then the music commenced—excellent music that set one's feet to jiggling, and the outsiders surged into the hall. . . . Before the Cross family could take up again the argument as to whether it should go Mr. Knowles ambled up to their chairs.

"Ma sent me out," he said. "She got it into her head maybe you folks would be kind of backward about goin' over on account of not bein' acquainted. I'll jest step over with you and make you known to two or three. Come right along."

He did not wait for them to accept or decline his proffered chaperonage, but waddled down the steps, evidently expecting to find them at his heels.

"Well!" exclaimed Janet again.

"Oh, come on. What's the difference?" Sarah said *sotto voce*. Then she chuckled. "Maybe he'll ask us to dance," she whispered, and giggled again at a conception so utterly absurd.

Mr. Knowles marched up the steps and elbowed his way through good-naturedly to the ticket window. "Here you be," he said, indicating with a pudgy hand. "Git your tickets right here. Fifty cents apiece. . . . Hey, Ab, fetched you some customers. We'll commence right here, folks. This is Ab Knuckles that runs the dances. Mr. and Mrs.

Cross, and their sister. Kind of see to it they have a good time."

Janet's face was hot with embarrassment; Sarah was not embarrassed, but was fearful of giggling in somebody's face. Mr. Knuckles jerked his reddish head and bent his gray eyes upon them. "Most got better acquainted with these ladies 'n I wanted to," he said without a trace of a smile. "They helped Eunice almost to run over me this mornin'. Don't hold it against them though." He extended a tanned sinewy hand to Warren and shook silently. He turned again to the ladies. "Don't think she did it a-purpose this time," he said gravely; "but she'd like to."

"What an extraordinary thing to say," Janet said in her most aloof manner.

"So 'tis," replied Knuckles. "So 'tis. Extraordinary situations call for extraordinary sayin's. . . . Step right in and sit anywheres that isn't occupied."

They passed on into the hall, now well filled with dancers and spectators, and were conscious of a pleasant surprise—not at the appearance of the people who were there but at the hall itself. It was a splendid room, not the work of a carpenter, but of an architect who knew and loved the Colonial. There was about it a certain dignity, a graceful severity which spoke eloquently of the character of those who had caused it to be erected.

At the distant end was a stage upon which the orchestra was playing; on either side of the pro-

scenium arch was a list of names in dignified letter-
ing, that at the right being the roll of Colchester men
who had fought in the Revolution, that at the left
those who had gone away from their homes to the
Civil War. Down each side of the hall were narrow,
lofty windows with panels between. Pictures seemed
to be hung in these panels, not paintings, but as
nearly as the Cross family could tell from a distance,
photographs in frames and daguerreotypes in cases.
And so they discovered them to be. Dozens of pictures in each section, men and women, and each section represented a family—a family which had
resided in Colchester for generations, back into those
days when the Green Mountain Boys fought under
Ethan Allen, when committees of public safety met
and conferred—back to those days and earlier. Before the dawn of the republic these men and women
had lived and labored here, hewing out their mountain farms, planting their orchards, building their
remote homesteads. It was impressive; it was a fine
thing to see assembled there all these faces of an elder
generation. And when one came to scrutinize those
faces—if his eye were an understanding eye and his
heart a perceiving heart—the impression became
profound and moving.

There was a similarity of feature. Splendid old
women with strength in every line of every feature,
strangely bearded old men with splendid brows and
firm lips and lean cheeks and stern eyes—a gray-

eyed race, it seemed. One could tell from those photographs that the majority of eyes were gray.

Here was something the Cross family never had encountered before, and they were not able yet to recognize what it was they saw. Janet and Sarah used the word "quaint," and found in the jet bonnets and ruching and chin whiskers and queer cravats matter for smiles. But even though they smiled, they were impressed. They must be impressed, for they were standing in the presence of something impressive, fine, noteworthy. Here was a village with a past of which it was conscious and of which it was proud. It knew from whom and from what it had sprung, and could estimate the value of its ancestors. Here was a certain tradition, and as one looked about the room, there were faces there which matched the faces upon the wall; young faces which would increase in strength until they would be worthy to set side by side with those ambrotypes which peered down upon them so gravely, so sternly. Here, in short, was race, the race to which America owes itself, the race which is the backbone of the nation.

To the Cross family it was only an experience, a novelty. They did not know, for they had never traveled and observed, that here was a sort of mother lode, a point of origin, from which streams of emigration had carried the fine gold westward and ever westward. They did not know that here was a typical American village, typical to the point of being a supreme example. Men and women from townships like Colchester had peopled the Middle West. Ohio was full of towns, some of almost equal antiquity, which matched Colchester in thought and in action; Michigan farmers are but transplanted New Englanders, thinking New England thoughts, speaking the New England idiom. And so of Indiana and Illinois and Iowa and the rest. Wherever you find unmixed American strain, there you find a town which acts and thinks and feels and talks as Colchester does. . . . An epitome of America!

Eunice Perrigo spied the Cross family as it entered with Mr. Knowles, and stopping her partner in the dance, led him to meet them. She nodded to the hotel man and spoke a rather breathless welcome to Janet and Sarah.

"This," she said, "is my brother James. I don't know how we come to be dancing together. Perrigos never do anything together. But here we are. . . . How do you do, Mr. Cross? James came in from the woods and I met him here. We didn't come together—you mustn't think that."

James Perrigo and Warren Cross eyed each other. It would have been difficult to confront with each other two men who were less alike in thought, in training, in outlook and in ambition—yet they looked not unlike. Both were tallish and slender, both clean cut of feature and intelligent of face; but James Perrigo possessed a stringy leanness, a grace which was apparent in every motion, a litheness which made one imagine him as always poised for instant motion.

His brown eyes—and they were fine eyes when one caught them in repose—were restless but not contented. His face impressed one as being drawn as your athlete's face is drawn when he is at the zenith of his training, at that point where one more ounce will carry him over the line to staleness. His cheeks were wind-and-sun tanned, so that it seemed they must crackle like brown paper if he smiled, and his teeth were extraordinarily white.

He did not smile; nor, confronted by two ladies dressed in the mode and by a young man carefully tailored, did he seem conscious of his own lack in that respect. His shoes were heavy and not polished; he still wore the flannel shirt, blue, with which he had come from the woods, and it seemed he must have bought the first suit the clerk showed him. Yet he was a handsome figure, inscrutable of face, with something untamed, restless, potential for good or evil about him. . . . Brown eyes! They seemed almost black as he returned Warren's scrutiny—and he did not smile.

"How do you do?" was his greeting, uttered in a singularly low and pleasant voice—a voice with a hush in it as if he were used to silences and given to listening for something which was difficult to hear.

"I'm hoping," Warren said, "that you'll find time within the next few days to show me about the camps."

Perrigo's eyes had rested with curious intentness upon Sarah's face, and he seemed to move them with an effort back to Warren. "The camps—yes," he said abstractedly. It conveyed nothing, either willingness to act as guide or resentment at being asked. Then his eyes moved back again to Sarah, who flushed and bit her nether lip.

"Will you dance?" he asked abruptly.

"Why—you're dancing this with your sister, aren't you?"

"Go ahead," said Eunice. "I'm glad to be rid of him. Perrigos are never good company for each other. . . . Heavens, there comes Walter through the door! Dance with me, Mr. Cross, before he comes up. I couldn't stand it if we got to be a family party."

Warren looked at Janet and lifted his brows, but there was nothing for it but to comply. However, Mr. Knowles stepped valiantly into the breech. "Let's you 'n' me step off," he said to Janet; and without waiting for her acceptance, clasped her waist with a pudgy hand and swept her away. He jiggled some and endowed the dance with more of the quality of the ancient waltz than she ever had experienced. Yet he danced well, and her fears for the integrity of her feet diminished with their progress about the hall. But her self-consciousness did not vanish. Dancing with this country hotelkeeper! It was absurd! She was angry, felt she was being made to appear ridiculous. But Mr. Knowles enjoyed himself thoroughly, utterly unaware in the kindliness of his intention of the chilling silence.

Abner Knuckles stood in the entrance way, watching. His eyes followed Eunice Perrigo about the room, then turned to rest, with a queer, questioning look, upon James, and came to halt upon the round, bald head of Walter Perrigo, who himself stood with his back against the wall, staring at his sister. Knuckles studied the man with curious intentness, noted the sparse hair over his ears, his slight mustache and drooping shoulders and the hint of a paunch which was making its appearance under his belt. It was a round, expressionless face, one without lines and creases, and yet it was not fat—expressionless if one did not dwell upon the eyes. But Knuckles was watching Walter's eyes, and he saw how they narrowed as Eunice floated past him in the dance, saw how they glinted with some malignant emotion, seemed to burn with a smoldering fire.

The elder Perrigo was unconscious that he was under scrutiny, and lost himself utterly in whatever emotion it was which possessed him. There was nothing of his brother and sister in him, in his face or figure or bearing. He seemed soft, planned by Nature for indoor uses, to live and move under a roof and shut in by walls. There was nothing of his brother's grace or that untamed feral alertness. There was nothing of that nervous energy and restlessness. Nor was there a hint of his sister's vivacity or that hunger for life, for something unexpressed and unidentified, which seemed always to be moving her to quick motion and a flood of words. Walter seemed a grayish, characterless sort of individual, incapable of keen pleasure or deep suffering or moving emotions—until one watched his eyes. They did not belong in that bland, rotund face.

Knuckles saw him pluck his eyes away from his sister as if they could not bear to abandon the scrutiny of her, saw them search the room, until they rested upon James—with a different expression, an expression not unlike Knuckles' when he had looked at James. It was a puzzled look, as if there was something about his brother which he did not understand, some puzzle he was trying to solve. So one might look at another to whom he contemplated putting some crucial proposition, wondering how it would be received, whether it would be well to make the proposition at all.

One thing a stranger might have gathered from those eyes of Walter Perrigo—he hated his sister. But Knuckles had known this. It was no surprise to him. Nevertheless, it received the impetus of a fresh interest in view of the arrival in Colchester of Warren Cross. The sending of a new manager to supplant Walter and James at this time renewed to keenness Knuckles' interest in the Perrigo family, but more especially in that concealed, unnatural hatred of Walter for Eunice.

Strange emotions, amazing manifestations of the nature of men and women, are to be found in your great and crowded cities. But if you would see strange things, amazing comedies and bleak tragedies, go to your little village. Look within neatly painted houses set back among maples, and amid broad green lawns if you would comprehend how puzzling, how contradictory, how deep and black and turgid may run the stream of human nature. Your villager may laugh more loudly, but he may also hate more deeply, and be urged on and on by his hatred to actions which, to the normal mind, seem to pass the border line of sanity. Monstrous skeletons hide away in the dust of village attics; bizarre drama moves its distorted figures along shaded streets and through commonplace, sunlit doorways to fantastic climaxes.

Knuckles moved slowly over to stand just behind Walter. Presently he spoke, after that habitual clearing of his throat. "Hello, Walt," he said.

Perrigo turned his round face. His eyes were bland now, and expressionless. "Evening, Ab," he replied.

No casual observer would have thought these two men to be the custodians of an inherited enmity, nor that the legacy had grown under their individual husbandry into a stark, coldly glowing animosity, the more bitter, the more dangerous, for being so well subjected.

"I see the new manager's come," Knuckles said.

"Seems as though," Walter answered.

Then Knuckles turned his back and walked slowly to take up again his position in the door. It did not seem this slight exchange of words had been worth the trouble. But Knuckles seemed to feel it had not been a waste of time.

CHAPTER V

THE Colchester venture had worn the aspect of an adventure, unreal and temporary, until the furniture arrived. But with the coming of the baby-grand piano and the dining-room table it took on an aspect of grim permanence. On that day when the curtains were hung and the rugs were in place, and the first meal was served in their new home, the Cross family realized depressingly that it had actually been transplanted from its native soil and that it was doomed to flourish, exotic, in this alien atmosphere.

The house was light, roomy, pleasant. The view from its piazza was one city dwellers would willingly have paid exorbitant board to witness upon their vacations, but here was no vacation. It was so quiet. Everything about it reminded them constantly of their beloved New York—reminded them by the absence of all those things to which they had been accustomed. One could lie in bed and hear the non-presence of the Elevated. The lack of an encircling city emphasized itself in every glance out of the window at limitless reaches of uninhabited green. Instead of fire escapes one regarded a lifting hillside of hardwood from the back windows, and nowhere did crowding walls of brick and stone obstruct the view. They missed that natural feeling of being

pent in and knew a lonely feeling as of being sus-
pended in space.

"You can see so far," said Janet plaintively.

"And the darn birds," said Sarah. "They get in
that tree outside my window and holler at five o'clock
in the morning."

"At home," said Janet—and she emphasized home
—"all one had to do was step outside the door and
you were some place. You were in the street; you
were in New York. There were people and shop
windows and theaters to go to if you wanted, and—
oh, you were just conscious of something to do, even
if you didn't want to do anything."

"When Ren gets home tonight I'm going to make
him stamp around and play the phonograph upstairs
while I lie on the davenport here, as if he were the
noisy family in the apartment above. It'll feel so
homelike."

"Anyhow that girl seems to be able to cook."

"But she's no more idea of serving than a cow."

The doorbell rang and, after a slight delay, Nellie
came in wiping her hands. She was a large girl
and friendly, awkward and strange with these city
people with whom she had come to live, but patheti-
cally anxious to please.

"Do you want I should go to the door, Mis' Cross?"
she asked.

"Certainly, Nellie."

They heard the door open and then listened with
confused emotions to a brief conversation.

"Why, hello, Nellie. I heard you were working here."

"Hello, Kitty. Hello, Edna. Come right in. The folks is to home. . . . Yes, pa cal'lated he could spare me."

"I didn't see you at the sociable last night."

"No, I walked over to my aunt's and sat with her."

"She's poorly this summer."

"Ever since she slipped and fell that time. . . . They're right in here."

Janet's cheeks were flushed with embarrassment, and she bit her lips; Sarah suppressed a giggle. If these callers were anybody, what must they think? On the contrary how could they be anybody if they commenced their call by exchanging amenities with the servant?

Nellie appeared leading the callers, two young women modestly but becomingly dressed, the one plump and dark, the other of excellent figure, pleasant, intelligent face and red hair. Janet and Sarah arose and stood nonplused while Nellie performed the office of introduction.

"Mis' Cross, let me make you acquainted with Mis' Bridge and Mis' Fox. An' *Miss* Cross."

"How do you do?" Janet said, with what graciousness she could muster in this appalling situation, and then rather sharply: "That will do, Nellie." Nellie nodded her friendliest to the callers and started to withdraw, but the lady with the red hair spoke to her again: "Tell your aunt I'm coming over to see her just as soon as I can."

"She'll be awful glad to see you, Edna."

"Won't you sit down?" asked Janet. "Or would you rather go out on the porch?"

"This is very nice," said the plump caller. "You are lucky, Mrs. Cross, to get a girl like Nellie."

"Yes, indeed," said Mrs. Bridge. . . . "Oh, before I forget it, here's a mess of asparagus. I cut it just before we came over. And, of course, you have no garden yet. I call myself a garden widow. That's the nearest approach we have to a golf widow here. The minute Henry's home from the bank he's out fussing with his vegetables."

Janet stood awkwardly with the paper-wrapped parcel in her hand, at a loss what to do with it and with the situation. She was conscious that her sister was eying her sardonically, which did not add to her self-possession.

"Thank you so much," she said; and then to be even with Sarah: "would you mind handing this to Nellie, please?"

Mrs. Fox's eyes were twinkling. "I suppose it does seem funny to you for your callers and your maid to be calling each other by their first names," she said, "but most of us here went to school together and played together as children. You'll find it won't interfere a bit with Nellie's cooking. Her father owns a fine farm over east of town, and the aunt she was speaking of—Mrs. Paget—is the widow of the president of the bank."

"And yet she goes out as a servant?"

"We don't say servant much in Colchester." No one in the world could mistake this for a rebuke. "Lately we've taken to calling them maids, which shows what education can do for one, but mostly they are hired girls."

"Nellie's younger sister is at the state normal now," said Mrs. Bridge. "I graduated there, but I never taught. You taught a year, didn't you, Edna?"

"Two. High-school Latin." She, it appeared, owned allegiance to the coeducational state university.

Janet was uncomfortable; it was hard for her to accustom herself to the fact that these young women —who exchanged first names with her cook, and whom she had been prepared to accept and to make allowances for as products of this remote village— were both better educated than she.

"Don't misunderstand me," she said. "We are here and it seems we shall be here for years, so we are determined to like it. But it is all so strange and so different. We're not adjusted yet. Tell me, didn't you find it frightfully dull and lonely here after you came back from college?"

"Why, no; at least I didn't," answered Mrs. Fox. "But we were born here, you see. I know how you feel. Of course, I've never lived in New York, but

I was there for six weeks once, and"—she smiled deprecatingly—"I didn't know how to act. Standards were so different. It wasn't dull exactly, but somehow there was nothing to do."

"Nothing to do in New York!"

"Of course, there were places to go, and it was exciting at first, but nothing to do as I have been used to doing. There everybody depends upon outside things for their pleasure—theaters and the like. Here we are used to being thrown upon our own resources. We make our pleasure. It rather seemed to me as if New Yorkers had lost the knack of it, as if their inward resources were dormant and they had to buy their enjoyment at so much a ticket or do without. . . . I was frightfully glad to be back again."

"We have lots of fun," said Mrs. Bridge. "There are half a dozen young couples here who flock around together most of the time. That's really why we came so soon and before you had time to get settled. They're coming to my house tomorrow night, and we'd love to have you. Maybe you'll sing for us. We've heard you have a lovely voice, and everybody's so excited about it."

"Thank you; I'm sure we shall love it."

"We've noticed you driving with Eunice Perrigo," Mrs. Fox said to Sarah. "I'm glad. She's such a restless piece it'll be good for her to have a girl to play around with, poor child."

"Why does everyone seem to sympathize with Miss

Perrigo?" Sarah asked. "She seems to need sympathy less than almost anybody else here."

"She's a peculiar child. Notional, as you might say, and inclined to be reckless. And no home life, of course. Mother and father dead—and there's a reason for sympathy just at this time, when she needs a mother most."

"She seems to do very well," Sarah said with a trace of flippancy.

"And, of course, her brothers," said Mrs. Fox. "She doesn't get on with Walter, and James—well, James is James. You have to take him or leave him. Sometimes I think he must be half Indian."

"I shan't be easy in my mind," said Mrs. Bridge, "until Eunice marries and settles down."

They got up presently, and though Janet pressed them to stay for tea, they declined. "This was just a little call, to say welcome to Colchester. But let's not be formal after this. And you'll come tomorrow evening," said Mrs. Bridge.

"Thank you. It was nice of you to come."

Then they were gone. Janet and Sarah watched them step into a little runabout and drive away.

"Well," said Sarah, "that's that. You're launched in society! I gather I was not invited to this hectic soirée. Young married couples only! I'm going out and be afraid of snakes!"

She went down the steps and out to the road—not deep with mud, its ruts filled with yellow water as she had first seen it, but dry, sun-baked, dusty—and crossed it to the bowlder-strewn slope which fell away to the river below. Even in this season of drying springs and dwindling brooks, its voice was audible, pleasantly audible, above the song of the locusts, pronouncing endlessly and metallically the letter Z. The voice of a mountain river is an interesting voice; rather the voice of a choir than of a soloist. It is made up of an infinitude of sounds—a sustained undertone of surge and rush and power, splashing, rippling, lapping, and now and again a tinkling as of little bells gently titillated. It is very difficult to be lonely beside such a stream, or to be afraid.

Sarah did not descend to its edge, bordered with witch hopple and river pinks and sumac, but seated herself with city-bred care upon a rock in the lee of a clump of ambitiously growing spruce and looked suspiciously about the neighborhood of her feet for signs of creeping or crawling or flying things. She had not come there to enjoy what Nature spread before her eyes, but rather, as she herself would have put it, to get the most good out of a grouch.

The call of Mrs. Bridge and Mrs. Fox had depressed her. It seemed, somehow, to affix the seal of finality upon their residence in Colchester and to make it an accomplished, irrevocable fact, as it had never been before. She could feel Colchester dragging at her, tugging her into itself with intention to make her as it was. She could see it reaching out for her sister; and she feared that ennui, sheer desperation, would drive her to let herself go—to sag, to

abandon her urban ideals in the effort to snatch
what pleasures were going. She saw herself forming
the sociable habit—the ice-cream-and-strawberry-
festival habit—and the visiting habit; she saw herself
losing that smartness for which she had always
striven, that smartness of dress and manner and of
speech which made her a New Yorker of New
Yorkers.

She saw today more emphatically than she had
seen before with the eyes of Broadway, of Fifth Avenue, of Times Square and Forty-second Street. In
short, she gave a private and very satisfactory dem-
onstration of that provincialism and circumscribed
vision which has become so profitably fashionable in
the city of culture and refined tastes, where one will
pay a hundred dollars for a seat at the première of
a theatrical performance in the hope of seeing an
apocrypha nude young lady immersed in a bathtub
of synthetic wine.

She sat brooding upon the unhappiness of her lot
when, suddenly, she was conscious she was not alone
—a shadow laid itself over her shoulder and made
an irregular pattern upon her lap. She had heard
no sound of approach, but one seldom did hear James
Perrigo when in motion.

Sarah started and turned with that apprehension
which your city-bred woman always shows of every
movement or sound in the country. There stood
James, dressed exactly as he had been at the dance
a few days before, unsmiling, a little saturnine pos-

sibly, but undeniably a fine figure of a young man.
He nodded and then stood motionless and silent—not
clumsily silent, but none the less still for all that.

"You startled me," she said.

He nodded again and let his eyes fall. Sarah was
not sure if his inability to meet her gaze engendered
a tiny suspicion, as her reading had told her it should
do, or if it were only a sign of diffidence, for he sat
down with a sleek, graceful movement, perfectly com-
posed, and let his eyes rove downward toward the
river.

"Well," she said, "why don't you say something?"

He lifted his eyes and let them drop again suddenly. "I hadn't thought of anything to say," he
answered.

She had a curious feeling that if she were to move
suddenly there would be an affrighted whir of wings
and he would disappear into the tree tops, or the
whisk of a tail and he would scurry into a hole among
the stones. So she sat very still, beginning to be a
bit uncomfortable, and wondered what to do next.
Apparently his intent was social, for he had settled
himself comfortably with the evident intention of remaining. Presently he said, with his eyes still upon
the distance, "I thought you would come out—some
time."

The implication of that was arresting. "Do you
mean you've been waiting for me to come out?" He
nodded. "And this is a call? But if you wanted to
call on me, why didn't you come to the house?"

"I didn't want to see you in a house," he said.

"Is it the custom here for men to wait around for young ladies to come out?"

A lift of the shoulders was his only answer to this, but it was eloquent; it seemed to convey his utter lack of interest in the customs of this place or of any other. While she searched for some line of conduct with which to meet the situation he continued to sit as if unconscious of her presence; but of a sudden she saw animation in his eyes and his finger lifted in an unhurried gesture to point. She peered in that direction and saw, two hundred yards away, a red fox, poised daintily, one forefoot lifted, sharp nose pointed to sniff the air. Presently the little creature satisfied himself with his surroundings and trotted away with that curious tiptoeing, ground-spurning, eye-satisfying gait which belongs to Brother Reynard.

"Was that a wild fox?" she asked.

"Yes."

"Are there many of them around?"

"Lots."

"Are they dangerous?"

He lifted his eyes to hers for an instant and dropped them again. In them was no hint of merriment; only a grave scrutiny as if he wished to satisfy himself of the good faith of her question. "To hens," he said.

She determined to find out how long it would be before he spoke of his own accord; it resolved itself into a contest of which he was unaware. He irritated her, yet he interested her; her social education had not equipped her to deal with a situation or individual like this. She contemplated getting up and leaving him abruptly; but she did not go, and the thought entered her mind that she might arouse him to a show of barbaric enthusiasm by showing him the mirror in her vanity case or letting him handle her string of gayly colored beads. Then she remembered he was Eunice Perrigo's half brother, a young man of wealth, graduate of a university. These matters added up to a total which she could not read. . . . His profile was fine, somewhat hawklike, but splendidly chiseled. He was so obviously contented with the way things were going.

"For goodness' sake," she said testily, "say something."

"Knuckles," he said, and flung his hand toward the river.

She glimpsed, between the clumps of witch hopple, the figure of a man wading up the stream—an eccentric thing to do.

"What's he doing?" she asked.

"Fishing. He'll stop there." James pointed to the spot below, where Knuckles would stop.

"Why?"

"No good beyond."

She watched to see if James was right, hoping contrarily he would be wrong. But he was not wrong. Knuckles emerged from the stream below and made toward them over the broken rock-strewn slope, busying himself with his rod and easing the creel which hung over his shoulder. He was not in waders, but had tied about his ankles the bottoms of his trousers legs and was wet to the waist. Presently he looked up and saw them, but gave no sign of recognition until he was almost abreast; then he nodded dryly, if a nod may be dry. Almost anything about Knuckles seemed to possess the quality of dryness.

"Miss Cross," he said, displaying his reddish hair. He had lifted his hat; but Sarah felt, and rightly, that it was not in deference to her. It had been a measure of coolness. "And James! Fraternizing! See you're doin' some summer loggin'."

James' face was still, and Sarah felt it to be hostile. He jerked his thumb downstream. "Been in?" he asked.

"Fished in yesterday, fished out today."

"Fished." James pronounced the word flatly, without inflection, but apparently it conveyed a desired meaning to Knuckles.

"Call it 'fished,'" he said. Then to Sarah: "Talked you most to death, has he?"

"We've been doing nicely, thank you," she said with some asperity.

"Seems as though," said Knuckles; then he, too, fell silent. These silences seemed a habit of those indigenous to this soil. His live gray—or were they blue?—eyes seemed engrossed in a detailed study of

James. James appeared unconscious of the scrutiny; his eyes searched the distant uplands.

"Miss Cross," Knuckles said presently, "there's pigeonholes for folks. You've got a pigeonhole and Walter's got a pigeonhole and Mr. Cross's got a pigeonhole. You can take 'em and slip 'em right into their own place. But James here—he's just clutterin' things up; there don't seem to be a pigeonhole he fits into. Anyhow I ain't been able to locate it. I got four-five picked out, but none of 'em quite suit."

James lifted his eyes and dropped them again swiftly. It was the only sign he exhibited of consciousness of this raillery—or was it raillery, Sarah wondered.

"There's the babe-in-the-wood pigeonhole." Knuckles shook his head. "Seems kind of likely sometimes. . . . There's the wicked-brother pigeonhole, and there's grounds for veerin' toward it. And there's the hand-in-glove-with-Walter pigeonhole— that's got possibilities. . . . I bought the cider mill day 'fore yesterday. Fetch down your apples this fall, James." He jerked his head abruptly and kept on his way to the road, down which he turned toward the village.

"Well!" exclaimed Sarah.

James said nothing. Presently he got to his feet; not, as the ordinary man does, by a series of pushes and heaves, but surely, lithely, in one flowing motion.

"Got to go now," he said.

"Do come again," she said ironically.

His eyes flicked upward to meet hers for an instant. "I will," he said.

When he had passed from sight Sarah got up from her rock frowning. "Well!" she said again. It was the best her vocabulary could do to cope with that episode.

CHAPTER VI

WARREN CROSS did not have to go to the dictionary to find the meaning of the word "exasperation." He was engulfed in it. Yet there was nothing overt upon which he could seize to raise an issue and clear the air. Sometimes he felt as if he were an ornamental fish, swimming in a bowl filled with hostility instead of water; but it was inert hostility. The results of it were apparent, but the method by which the results were obtained was as difficult to discover as the germ of some obscure disease.

It was a sort of disease, and the business was sick of it. The more he went about it, in his diplomatic way, to discover what was wrong, the more he became convinced that his company had made a bad bargain. Yet all the elements of a good bargain were present—an excellent plant in good condition, fine timber and plenty of it, favorable railroad rates to the markets, satisfactory wages to the labor. But these added up to a monthly loss.

As any good business man would do he had given his first attention to the matter of overhead. Many a promising business has been eaten up by that ravenous creature. But this particular overhead did not have to show a Gargantuan appetite. There had been a full run of logs, but the inventories of the past year showed a distressingly high percentage of Number 3 Common after the saws had done their work. Though labor costs were low, production was low also—and woods costs were high. Warren could discover no reasons.

From the beginning he had been painstakingly considerate of Walter Perrigo; he did not have to be considerate of James, for that young man was as hard to lay hands on as a frightened deer. . . . He came home on the evening of Mrs. Bridge's party in a state of mind, following a conference with the suave Walter.

"Mr. Perrigo," he said, "I have been going over the books of this concern for a period of years. When the mills were owned by your family there was an average profit of from eight to ten thousand dollars a month."

"About that," said Walter.

"Six months after the Consolidated took over, this showing dropped and has been dropping ever since, until there is none left. General conditions have changed little—even the management has been the same. I wish you would tell me frankly to what you attribute it."

"Aftermath of the war," said Walter.

"Production has dropped."

"Men won't work as they used to."

"The percentage of high grade to low grade lumber has decreased."

"We've been cutting on those ridges," Walter said, "and have had a run of bad timber."

"It costs us 2 to 30 per cent more to fell a tree and haul it to the mill."

"That," said Walter, "is James' department. I'd rather you discussed it with him."

"But you buy the camp supplies and make the contracts."

"On James' requisitions," Walter said.

It was baffling. Exasperation ate like rust into the metal of Warren's self-control, but no sign of it was visible to Walter's bland but watchful eye.

"Have you no suggestions?" he asked presently.

"I've been trying to work it out for a year," Walter said. "Personally I believe it is just a temporary condition, and we'll work out of it after a while."

That was the gist of it; nothing tangible—inertia. Simply a lack of results. Warren had studied Walter sharply and found the man knew his business. He was efficient; he was a capable mill man. Indeed, as a manufacturer, Warren recognized him to be far better equipped than himself.

"We're not the only mill to run into it," Walter said. "The Grainger Brothers—busted this spring. The banks are carrying Whittaker. Oregon fir is coming around by boat, riding into Eastern markets cheaper than we can lay down our own stuff."

"But we're cutting hardwood," said Warren.

"And spruce. I lay our loss to the spruce. Show

me a mill that's made money on spruce for a year or two."

"Would you recommend cutting out the spruce next year?"

"I'd go slow. I'd go slow everywhere. Can't tell what the market'll do."

That was always Walter's counsel—to go slow, to sit tight, to carry on and wait for something to turn up—and it was not Warren's way to wait. He had not been sent there by his superiors to wait, but to act. Results, profits, were demanded of him, and that without delay. He got up and went back to his own office, where he sat reflecting, and was not happy.

While he sat at the dinner table that evening he talked it out. Always he could clear up his thoughts and make them cohere by putting them into words, and Janet, though she did not always understand clearly, was a partisan listener.

"You haven't been here long enough to do anything," she said in his defense.

"I'm beginning to think I can't stay here long enough to do anything—in the conditions that are there."

"Then change the conditions," she said.

"I'd have to clean house, and I don't want that. The company doesn't want that. The goodwill of the place where your mill is located is a mighty good thing to have. But I'm afraid it will come to that. It would make things difficult for us though. We'd be as popular here as a wasps' nest at a strawberry festival."

"It's not so gorgeous here anyhow," said Sarah.

"Yes, but folks are friendly. I gather you don't care much whether they are or not; but believe me, ladies, it would make a heap of difference. Now they want us to enjoy ourselves and be in things. Maybe the things aren't what we want to be in, but they are all we have. Now suppose I were to make a clean sweep, as I'm afraid it will come to—fire Walter and James, get rid of the minor executives and superintendents and discharge half the crew. We'd have the whole town about our ears. Most of them look at their jobs as something they own—vested rights. I'll bet half the people we meet tonight are connected with the mill, either actually or by blood or marriage."

"The quicker," said Janet, "you can do your job, the quicker we can clear out of this place."

"That mill," Warren said, "was a little gold mine. Why in blazes did the Perrigos ever sell it?"

"It wasn't the Perrigos," said Sarah; "it was Perrigo—so Eunice says. Walter did it. Eunice has had a grouch about it ever since."

"And where did James stand?"

"Nobody," said Sarah, "seems to know. James," she said reflectively, "is a queer egg. He's the sort of fish they ought to exhibit in a tank. I can't recite on James; I'm not prepared."

"What do you know about him, sis?"

"He called on me—if you can call it that. It was grand, but it wasn't war. As a caller James is a novelty, and some other poor little rich girl can have my share of him. He's not fluent, but he loves the wild flowers. If you were to shut us in a room together for the evening only one would come out alive, and if it was me, I'd be a raving lunatic."

"He made a hit with you, didn't he?"

"Anyhow he made an impression. He'd do for a statue of the great silent places. But all the same my acute little brain got the impression James had all his buttons. That funny man Knuckles came along ——"

"Did he call on you too?"

"No, he was bringing the fish home from pasture, and he found me sitting on a rock, while James impersonated another rock. He chaffed James a bit, as the English say, but didn't get a rise. Imperturbable James! I gathered from Mr. Knuckles' remarks that James was a deep, dark mystery to him also."

"You'll see him tonight," said Janet. "When Mrs. Bridge called up to be sorry about not making it clear you were invited, she said Eunice and James were coming."

"Awk!" said Sarah, and pretended to faint. "Well, I don't suppose he'll make it any worse. What'll they all do—play dominoes or clap in and clap out? . . . I never did care much for the Subway, but if I ever get back, I'm going to ride on it a whole day just for pleasure."

"They want me to sing, Ren," said Janet.

"Fine!"

"But what'll I sing—to a crowd like that?"

"You'll have to play your accompaniment on a melodeon," Sarah said. "Better stick to Gospel Hymns, if you know any, or Home, Sweet Home. If you spring any of that Italian stuff on them they'll probably think you've come down with hysterics."

Janet's eyes snapped. "I said I wouldn't let myself go if I came here, and I shan't. I'm going to keep what I've got. I won't lower my standards."

"Be a little missionary," said Sarah, "and elevate them. They'll love it. You tinker with their musical taste, and I'll show 'em the Charleston."

"For cat's sake, Janet," Warren said, with a wrinkle of apprehension between his eyes, "don't go high-hatting them all over the place!"

"I shan't. But I shan't play down either. I'll just be myself."

"Whoops!" cried Sarah in pretended delight.

"I'm going to dress," Janet announced, and Warren saw she was in a contrary humor, which did not make for his peace of mind.

"What d'ye mean—dress?" asked Sarah.

"I'm going to wear my orchid," said Janet.

"Kind of doggy, isn't it?" Warren asked dubiously.

"And you," said Janet, "are going to wear a dinner jacket."

"I'm not. Nobody'll be wearing them."

"Then they ought to," Janet said.

" 'Many an honest heart beats beneath a ragged coat,' " quoted Sarah. "What the well-dressed lady wears in Colchester!"

"I'm going to dress and act exactly as I should do if I were invited out at home," Janet said stubbornly.

Warren shrugged his shoulders helplessly. "Tear into it," he said, "but I'm going as is. I'd feel like a fool."

"And I," said Sarah, "shall dazzle society. Maybe they've never seen a lady's knees here, and mine are rather satisfactory. The younger set—that's me."

The family was not precisely in a merrymaking humor as they got into the car to start. Warren was apprehensive; Janet quivered with irritation which she took out upon her husband and rather looked forward to taking out on the company; and Sarah frankly said she was going slumming.

"I do hope the butcher will be there," she said with a giggle. "I find him quite charming. 'I raised the critter them steaks come off of,' he told us this morning, but he didn't mention her name. Maybe it was Buttercup."

Warren drove silently, but he could feel perversity exuding from his wife, who sat in the front seat beside him. She was lovely; that he had to admit, even though she had deliberately got herself up as for the jazziest of night clubs. As for Sarah she might have been a chorus girl with expensive tastes

—petite, pert, daring. Nor was she unarmed with the lip stick and its complementary weapons.

The home of the Bridge family, before which they presently came to a stop, was a white house standing upon a corner. Two large maples shaded its front, and the side yard sloped away toward the brook which flowed into the river a couple of hundred feet away, after passing under a little iron bridge. Beside the bridge was the public scale, across from it the blacksmithy, and above it the hill lifted steeply in tip-tilted pasture and woodland and sugar orchard. The village straggled up the slope, clinging desperately to the road, but behind that narrow ribbon of houses was farm land. Stone fences meandered, young spruces struggled up in mowings, diligently seeking to reclaim as forest what man had cleared with so much labor, and seemingly to so little purpose. If one stood upon the Bridges' broad side porch with back toward the town and the street, he saw nothing but hills and trees and rocks and solitude—and yet the house was almost in the center of the village. The public library occupied the opposite corner.

As for the house itself it was one of those rectangular buildings beloved by our grandfathers and great-grandfathers. The door was embellished with side and fanlights; its windows were sashes of eight panes in the ancient manner. From the rear a wing containing an enormous kitchen extended onward until it gave into a red barn, now transmuted into a garage. The lines were simple, sturdy; the proportions excellent. As architecture it was what our suburbs strive for and sometimes approach.

But those pilasters at the corners actually concealed eight-by-eight spruce timbers set in the framework a hundred and fifty years ago. They were not merely ornamental, not hollow simulations of reality. It was well kept, freshly painted. At the rear and on the side toward the brook were great clumps of lilacs, and behind one of these was a pile of chopped wood. A man named Bridge had erected this house when Washington was still President; a man named Bridge stood in the door this evening to welcome the Cross family as it descended from the company's automobile.

He came down the steps and the walk with hand extended, a round, pudgy young man with sandy hair and a coat which drew between the shoulders. New England was in his voice; not so much a matter of dropped letters as of tone and inflection.

" 'Light," he said, "and hitch. Glad to meet you, Mr. Cross." He beamed upon the ladies. "Come right in and make b'lieve you've been raised with us. How's things to the mill?" He waited for no reply and his voice lifted a key as if the very occupation of talking excited him, and he spoke so rapidly, and broke his sentences in two with teeth-showing laughs, that it was difficult to understand him.

"Everybody's here but you, but you got a right to be stylish once Pliny Smith lugged in his cello

and there's a couple of fiddles here give me your hat
and the ladies upstairs first door to the right." He
pronounced this without punctuation.

They heard laughter and talk subside suddenly
as they entered, and Mrs. Bridge came through the
parlor door to greet them and to lead Janet and
Sarah to the room above where wraps were left by
the guests. There followed a few minutes of stiffness
and formality, an awkward pause as those already
in the room took stock of the arrivals. Introductions,
then restrained talk while both parties strove to be
at their ease. Something more than a dozen young-
ish people were there, among whom Sarah, with relief, saw Eunice Perrigo—and, with a sensation which
was not quite relief, saw her brother James. Henry
Bridge found a place beside Janet, while his wife
took charge of Warren. Eunice moved over on the
sofa to make room between herself and a tall, stooping, rather pallid young man who turned out to be
Tom Hewitt, the local man of law. He smiled bash-
fully and crowded away as far as he could without
destroying the piece of furniture.

"What's the matter anyhow?" Henry Bridge demanded tactfully. "Everybody acts as if they were
just going to file past for a last look at the remains."

Janet was suddenly uncomfortable, self-conscious,
questioning her own good taste and blaming it upon
Colchester. She was the only woman there with
arms and neck uncovered—the only one, apparently,
to whom this gathering was a function. She saw

how wrong she had been to dress, but would not admit
it to herself; and she was unpleasantly conscious that
every woman in the room was trying with might and
main not to stare at her. It was worse than she
imagined it could be.

"Well," asked Henry genially, "how do you like
Colchester—as far as you've got?"

"I—it's rather strange yet," she said icily.

"I s'pose it is different," he said. "Never lived
in a city myself. Wouldn't know how to go about it.
Wouldn't want to, seems as though."

"No," said Janet, "I should imagine not."

He shot a quick look at her to see if there were a
sting in the tail of this, and color rose to his ears.
Janet was ashamed, which made her more difficult
to deal with than before.

"Now what did I do wrong?" Henry asked himself. He had been cautioned by his wife that the
Cross family might feel strange at first and that
he must be considerate of them. He had tried his
best to be considerate, but apparently with scant
success. He suffered from that queer self-consciousness which often overtakes your rustic dweller in his
contacts with city folks; not a feeling of inferiority,
exactly, for decidedly he does not feel inferior; but
an emotion mixed perhaps of a little envy and a bit
of resentment because he imagines the city person
feels superior.

"Hope you like your house. We call it the most
modern in town." This was his next effort.

"It will do very well—while we stay."

"Oh, I got the idea you were here for a long time
—a couple of years anyhow." He laughed uneasily.
"And anybody that stays here two years never wants
to go away again."

"I imagine I shall be an exception," Janet said,
and the conversation languished. Presently he excused himself on the pretext that he had to see to
something in the kitchen, and disappeared. A fat
young woman moved her bulk into the vacant chair
and lifted a pair of bright round eyes to Janet's
face. Janet strove to appear unconscious of her,
rather resented her drawing nearer. But when the
stout one spoke it was in so charming and so softly
modulated a voice that Janet turned to stare as if
she could not believe her ears.

"Mrs. Cross, I hope you won't mind my telling
you how lovely your dress is. I adore that shade!
But look at me—just look at me—and then imagine
me in orchid! . . . Is it true that you sing?"

"A very little," Janet said.

"I'm sure it is more than that. We all love music
here, and get to hear so little of it. . . . Tom and
I went down to Boston at Christmastime last year to
hear Paul Whiteman."

Janet bit her tongue. It was about what one
might expect. Paul Whiteman!

"I was amazed," said Mrs. Hewitt, for she was
the wife of the pale, thin, drooping young lawyer.
"I rather expected to hear something offensively

extravagant—you know—something blaring and awfully freakish." This, thought Janet, was a bucolic pose. She waited for more. "But I really think he has accomplished something notable. More than a pioneer usually accomplishes in the arts. I looked to find a crude, cheap Cézanne of music—a sort of cubic mountebank."

"And you found?"

"I don't like to give an opinion on such a matter to an accomplished musician, but it seemed to me he had found something new and big and expressive —a new thing to say and a new method of saying it. . . . I was fascinated." She stopped and laughed a trifle embarrassedly, and then said, with a charming inflection of humor: "And he was so fat. It was cheering to see a fat person accomplishing something."

Janet was interested in spite of herself. The woman might be classed as dowdy, but there was a certain appeal about her, an adipose charm—and intelligence,—something that might be mistaken for cultivated intelligence.

"Do you go often to Boston?" Janet asked.

"We can't afford it. We're country lawyers. And there's the baby. I got Mattie to stay with her tonight—Mattie's the little girl next door—but she holds me pretty close. Without help in the house, I can't get away much. Though I guess I don't want to get away any more. No, I'm kind of making a business of that baby."

"How old is she?"

"Twenty months." She was about to become expansive upon the subject of baby when her round eyes became suddenly larger. "Why," she exclaimed, "there's Ab Knuckles! What next? How ever did anybody get him to a party?" Then, Janet noticed, Mrs. Hewitt's eyes moved across the room to Eunice Perrigo and from her to James, and she gave her head a little shake as if there were something which caused her disquiet. "And it would have to be the one time the Perrigos are here!"

Janet watched the little episode with the keen interest which all women—and all men—feel in watching the conduct of other persons who find themselves in a difficult situation. That there was a situation at all did not seem to occur to Knuckles; he leaned against the doorcasing, tall, angular, not exactly saturnine, but some good-natured blood relation to saturnine. Certainly he was not handsome. He was carelessly dressed; his features were striking in the sense that Abraham Lincoln's homely features were striking, but he dominated the room. It may be he was a small toad in a tiny puddle, but in that company he was a personage.

He had not spoken since he came in, nor did he look as if it were his intention to speak at all. Somehow Janet received the impression that he had come just for the purpose of leaning silently against the wall, and that when he had had enough of that occupation he would go away again without having made himself audible.

She glanced at Eunice, on the sofa beside Sarah. Vivacity had deserted the girl's face, to be replaced with an expression of sullenness, and she eyed Knuckles slantwise. James, after one swift glance at Knuckles, remained imperturbable. James, thought Janet, was a handsome young man—or would be if she could have the handling of his sartorial affairs for a time—but probably dumb. She read his lack of expression as a lack of quick intelligence. There were many opinions of James, and certainly Janet was entitled to the one she selected.

"Good!" Mrs. Hewitt said. "Pliny Smith's getting out his cello. It's about time we were doing something and not sitting like bumps on a log."

"Who is Mr. Smith? A musician?"

"Runs the livery stable," said Mrs. Hewitt.

Livery stable and cello! Janet would have giggled at the incongruity of it if her humor had not been to find something distasteful in all she saw. She wondered if Turkey in the Straw could be played on that instrument.

"Mamma," shouted Henry Bridge, "where'd you put my bull fiddle? Looks like I mislaid it. You didn't pack it away with the best silver, did you? Eh?"

Janet could not know this was a time-honored joke of Henry's, but she didn't think much of it; and she wondered what a bull fiddle was and what she was going to have to suffer now. The incongruity of mislaying a bass viol was not likely to excite her humor this evening.

But presently, the viol discovered in a closet, a string quartet assembled itself—Henry and the livery man; Doctor Lowrie, a man with baggy trousers and mussed hair; and Tom Hewitt, the pale husband of the fat woman at Janet's side.

"Look out!" shouted Henry. "Give us room to swing 'em!"

"The boys love to play," said Mrs. Hewitt. "It's almost a vice with them, as cribbage is with the old men under the barber shop."

"If Tom ever gets that fiddle tuned right," said Henry loudly—he always spoke as if his auditors were a long way off—"we'll get to whizzin'."

"If I got to suffer," said a young man, whom Janet later discovered to be Larry Fox, the dry-goods man, "I'm goin' to do it in a cloud of smoke." He leaned across toward Janet and said in a stage whisper: "It's worse'n you can imagine it'll be. But you wait. When they get through I'll tell some conundrums and everybody'll have a good time."

"Shut up!" bawled Henry. "Dog-gone, I can't play with my coat on." He took it off and flung it upon a chair. "Ready, fellers? Then, one, two, three—shoot!"

Doc Lowrie lifted his bow in signal. Janet gritted her teeth and half closed her eyes. It might not be so bad if the room kept up its clatter to drown the

sounds which must issue from such a string quartet!
But the room ceased to clatter. It was an arrange-
ment from Butterfly. In the beginning Janet did
not listen to the music; she watched Henry, whose
pudgy body swayed in time to the music, and who,
catching her glance, actually grinned at her and
winked roguishly. He was having a gorgeous time
—and the execrable taste of the proceeding disgusted
her. Clowning! Clowning with music!

Then, in spite of herself, she listened. Butterfly!
They were actually playing it, not torturing it!
Like all people who know a little and unconsciously
have come to a pretense that they know more, Janet
had little real critical faculty. If the Flonzaleys
were playing she knew she was hearing something
superb; if some quartet of street musicians under
her window had played equally as well she would
not have known it was superb. More or less patronizingly she would have admitted it to be fair—on
the theory it was not remarkable they should play
well, but marvelous they should play at all.

They were done. Janet was puzzled, nonplused.
It could not be that good music had been produced
by those four uncouth, ridiculous men! But it had
seemed good. She wondered what ailed her. Then
she looked about the room. It showed none of the
boredom which yokels should exhibit in the presence
of that art—which should be the sole property of
God's chosen people, the intellectuals. They ap-
plauded as if they had enjoyed it; not with restraint,

as would have been becoming, but joyously, and with shouted comments.

"Tom must 'a' greased his bow tonight," said Larry Fox. "He didn't do the usual damage."

"Whale into another one," urged John Watts, the insurance man.

"What'll you have? Just name it. We got 'em all in stock. This orchestry can play anythin' from God Save the King to a Hot Time in the Old Town."

"How's that one by the feller that sounds like a harelipped Canuck tryin' to hiccup?" suggested Larry.

Evidently the quartet understood this description, for it moved gently into a thing which, with some small astonishment, Janet recognized as Tschaikovsky. At the end Henry made a parade of wiping his pink brow. "Gosh, fellers," he said, "that kind of gets up a sweat. . . . Say, sing something, Mrs. Cross. I'm plumb played out with sawin' wood."

She went to the piano without a word, not graciously, and not exactly patronizingly. Warren could read her thoughts. Without prelude, she sang a group of Russian folk songs; sang them daintily with sureness, making the most of her minor gift. Perversely she had chosen that group of songs as most likely to be unsuited to the taste of her audience. . . . Folk songs were quite the thing; just now everybody was going in for folk songs.

When she was done she sat facing the piano for a moment, a little apprehensive. No human being with a spark of the artist in his make-up but dreads to meet a lack of appreciation. She need have had no fears, though the applause was not such as she might have preferred.

"By, gosh, that was slick!" shouted Henry. "Welcome to our city."

She made as if to get up from the piano, but Larry Fox's voice protested. "Hey, Cross, ain't you got any control over your wife? Make her stay right there and give us some more."

Knuckles spoke for the first time: "I'd like to hear Rubinstein's Melody in F, seems as though," he said in his slightly nasal, deliberate voice.

"I'm afraid I can't play it," Janet said shortly.

Mrs. Hewitt heaved and billowed in her chair and finally achieved a stance. "I'll make shift to get through the accompaniment for you," she said, "if you'll promise to be kind of patient with me."

"That's the stuff, Mandy," roared Henry. "And jest bear down your heft on the loud parts."

Amanda Hewitt smiled good-naturedly and waddled toward the piano. Janet was appalled; with what dreadful fiasco was she confronted now? But there seemed to be no honorable avenue of retreat, so she surrendered the bench. Mrs. Hewitt ran her fingers over the keys tentatively, brushed back her sleeve and settled her massive bracelets; then she nodded amiably to Janet, who stood biting her lips nervously.

"Never mind if we break down," said Amanda. "Everybody'll know it's my fault."

But they did not break down. Amanda played —and she accompanied, which is a rare art, making Janet aware constantly of her support. It was an accompaniment which accompanied, marching along by her side a safe, dependable, self-effacing companion.

"You—you play very well," Janet said when the last note died away. Again she was astonished, and it must have shown in her eyes.

"Folks," said Amanda comfortably, "are always kind of surprised that a fat woman can do anything."

They moved away from the piano together. Janet glanced about for the man who had asked her to sing. Knuckles stood in the same place against the door, but he was not looking at her; his eyes, half shut, curiously intent and inquiring, rested upon James Perrigo. It seemed as if he had forgotten all about his request; at any rate he offered no thanks. Presently, without a word to anybody, he turned and left the house.

"That was a queer man who asked me to sing," Janet said to Amanda.

"Ab Knuckles. . . . Well, Ab is Ab, and that's all you can say about it. I guess, though, after all, he's about the most natural one of all of us. We're all kind of changed from what the last generation was, and the one before that. So's the world, I suppose. Everything's different, even up here in the hills—everything but Knuckles. He's like his father —like as two peas. He's what we all are at heart, but outside we've kind of got away from it—more's the pity."

"A typical New Englander, I suppose."

Amanda glanced at her quickly and shook her head. "A typical American, I'd put it."

That was the end of the music. The rest of the evening was difficult for Janet; it seemed to consist of refreshments and confusion. No attempt was made at entertainment. People sat about and talked, not quietly. Everyone seemed too healthy to be subdued. They traipsed into the kitchen to help; men found amusement in parading about in Mrs. Bridge's aprons. And there was no liquor. It had not been mentioned; apparently nobody thought of it. No cocktails, no bridge—and everybody enjoying himself! Janet was bored and showed it. Even when they organized some perfectly absurd charades and acted them with childish abandon, Janet was bored. She forgot she had enjoyed hugely no more intellectual charades a couple of months ago in a studio; she forgot that the cross-word-puzzle craze was born at evening parties of the *intelligentzia*.

She made her way to her husband and whispered, "When can we go home out of this?"

"We'll go as soon as it's decent," he said. Then: "Sarah seems to be having a good time." Sarah was. She was so young that she could still enjoy any admiration, and Eunice had not left her side during

the entire evening. They had whispered and giggled, unconscious of the rest; unconscious even of
James, who sat the evening through and scarcely
took his eyes off her.

"You've knocked James off his balance," Eunice
said. "He's been gaping at you all night. Well,
you can thank the Lord it isn't Walter. Imagine
Walter getting stuck on anybody—or Ab Knuckles!"

"I sort of like Mr. Knuckles' looks," Sarah said.
Eunice sniffed.

Janet stood over them. "We're going now," she
said. "Come along, Sarah."

"Oh, let her stay, Mrs. Cross," Eunice begged.
"I'll see she gets home—James and I. We're terrible
safe people, you know."

Janet shrugged her shoulders. "Stay if you want
to," she said, with an air which made clear her opinion of anybody who would want to stay.

"Your sister hasn't gone crazy over this party, has
she?" Eunice asked when Janet turned away. "Um
—if I were a loving sister I'd turn you over to
James. But I'm not a loving sister. Anybody in
town'll tell you that." She paused and her face dark-
ened. "I think I hate Walter," she said, and there
was no mistaking her tone for pretense. "I'm not
sure about James."

Sarah lived through an uncomfortable moment.
Eunice's intenseness disturbed her. Then her eyes
rested upon James' dark, finely chiseled face, and
she said to herself that nobody seemed sure about

James. Nobody seemed to know where James fitted into the picture. Nor was she able to answer that question herself, even after she had been driven home by Eunice and her brother. For James did not open his mouth to utter a single word except, "Good night."

CHAPTER VII

SQUIRE KNUCKLES sat at the head of the breakfast table, his son at the foot. In a dim light one would have had difficulty in telling which was which. This was not because the squire was younger than his years, nor Abner older. Eli Knuckles' years were visible upon his face, though not so perceptible in his tall spare figure—that body which he had given to his son. Abner was his father as the squire had been at something under thirty; the squire was Abner as Abner would be at something over seventy.

It was an old-time New England breakfast—flapjacks and maple sirup, salt pork with thick white gravy, fried potatoes, coffee, and, to make it complete and satisfactory, two kinds of pie were at hand, berry and apple.

The two men spoke little; a nod had sufficed them for greeting when they met after the night's rest. To the housekeeper they did not speak at all, but this did not hurt her feelings—she was used to it.

"You was to Bridges' last night," the old man said suddenly, not looking up from his plate.

"Dropped in," said Abner.

"What fur?"

"James Perrigo was there."

"Huh! So was his sister." There was a note of accusation in this. Abner nodded. "Harum-scarum," said the old man. Then he lifted his eyes and there was smoldering fire in them. "She's a Perrigo," he said. "Don't forget it."

"Ain't apt to," said Abner.

"I been watchin' ye," said the squire. "I've seen ye stand on the walk a-lookin' after her. If ye was to do anythin' now when matters is comin' to a head —anythin' to upset 'em—I cal'late I'd curse ye, Abner, and go into my grave cursin' ye."

"Ain't apt to," Abner said again.

"Let dog eat dog," the squire said.

"It goes against the grain to see dog eat kitten."

"She's a Perrigo kitten," the old man said. Then, his voice terrible in its vindictiveness: "The sins of the fathers shall be visited on the children." Abner nodded. "It was the way of the Almighty to destroy his enemies root and branch."

"I don't know as I always hold with the Almighty," said Abner.

"Many ways," said the old man, "you been a good boy, Abner. I hain't suffered grief by you. But it seems like ye don't fear God like I taught ye. Folks is slippin' away from their religion. Preachers hain't preachin' it. It's been long since I sat in church with the sweat of fear runnin' down my forehead. No matter how folks seeks to delude themselves, Abner, the's a hell, and a hell of burnin' pitch and brimstone."

"I ain't arguin' against it."

"Perrigo blood robbed me and Perrigo blood shall repay—wearin' sackcloth and ashes."

"I cal'late to make 'em pay in full," said Abner.

"Savin' and exceptin' none of 'em, but Walter fust of all."

"The main thing is to get our own back, seems as though."

"The main thing hain't dollars and cents—it's justice. And justice means punishment. If they was to walk in this day and make restitution to the last farthing, I wouldn't rest content."

"Seems as though," said Abner.

"I've lived my years in justice," the old man said solemnly. "No man kin point at me and say he didn't get from me his due, nor more than his due, nor less. . . . What's it to us if Walter—or Walter and James—robs this highty-tighty gal? Or wuss. With her paintin' and her gaddin' about and all, she's bound to come to a pass. . . . But I've watched ye starin' at her, Abner."

"I stare some at James and at Walter."

"But not the same. I hain't to be fooled nor deceived. . . . And as for James—I've noted you hold doubts in your mind regardin' James."

"And hold 'em yet," said Abner.

"It hain't needful. He's a Perrigo."

"I hold it is needful. We know what Walter aims to do, if we ain't clear as to the manner of it."

"He's deliverin' himself into our hands," said the squire.

"But if James is for him or against him—if James is aware, or if James is doin' his plannin'—that we don't know. Folks that don't study James miss a lot of education. . . . He's upset by that Cross girl that just come to town."

"What do ye conclude about the man Cross?"

"I conclude Walter's grippin' close to the end of his rope. Cross is citified and all, but he wouldn't have been sent to do this job if he hadn't been qualified. He's movin' deliberate, but he'll git at facts."

"Walter sold that mill—which was built up with money that belongs to me—because no man kin steal a mill. But it ain't so with money." Abner nodded. "And," said the old man, "he's been robbin' the mill and holdin' it back so as, when this comp'ny sees the's no profit to be made by it Walter kin buy it back for little with what he steals from his brother and sister."

"Or with what he and James steal from the girl."

"No matter."

"It's what I incline to believe. She got the biggest share. The house and farms was left to her alone, and a third of the rest. Walter hated her from the moment she was born, like he hated her mother when she married his father. He was a grown man then, Walter was. His feelin's toward James I ain't fathomed. He wan't but twelve when James was born."

"I recall him as a boy, and he wan't one to be

trusted. Slinkin', deceivin', lyin', as many'll remember. I cal'late Walter was as capable of evil at twelve as he is today, lackin' the years and the experience."

"His father trusted him," Abner said.

"Mebby," said Eli; "bein' as they was off the same piece of cloth. Still an' all, he didn't favor him in his will. He favored the girl."

"But made Walter guardian and trustee of the property."

"It was the Almighty, workin' in his mysterious way for their destruction," Eli said harshly.

"Don't seem to me," Abner said, "if I was the Almighty I'd have to resort to so much plannin'. Seems as though I'd step out and do."

"The ways of Providence hain't to be fathomed," Eli said reverently.

The old man finished his breakfast and moved back his chair; his severe, sturdy, splendidly chiseled old face was set in an expression of determination—such determination as is characteristic of men of his day and of older generations which we see in daguerreotypes. The hall beside the hotel was filled with them. A little grim, something thin of lip and stiff of neck. Hard men to sway from a chosen path, stubborn, perhaps, and harsh in their judgments, but strict in their will to give and to receive exact justice. Afraid of their emotions, mystic and yet material, scorning the æsthetic, afraid of the softer way; yet withal of splendid heart, capable of great loves and high friendships. Capable as well of disinheriting a be-

loved child for cause, or of sending a guilty friend
to the gallows. And having done so, of concealing
from mortal eyes the gaping, throbbing, gnawing
wound.

Knuckles did not lift his eyes from his plate as his
father moved to the door, and only glanced up briefly
as Eli paused upon the threshold to speak a final
word. "I seen you starin' after her," he said.

Knuckles finished his meal imperturbably and
arose, going through exactly the same movements
as his father. It might have been an imitation carefully rehearsed, but it was unconscious imitation—
that sort of imitation which causes a pea vine to produce peas as its ancestors did, instead of branching
out for itself to produce apples or corn or tomatoes.
He walked to the hall tree and put on his shabby hat
and then stood in the door for a moment considering.
Knuckles had no place of business, no office, no pro-
fession; yet he was busy and prosperous. He
thrived upon what other men overlooked—upon little
transactions if no large ones came to hand, upon
swaps and trades. He would buy a house or a hog;
dicker for a bundle of shingles or a hundred acres
of timber. He even hired himself out for the day
occasionally if nothing better came to hand. A dollar was worth making if a thousand dollars was not
to be had, and there was little he could not turn his
hand to from doctoring an ailing cow to a job of
carpentering. A Jack-of-all-trades, but who was
there to say he was master of none?

He was thinking about his father's pronouncement. It was true, he had stared after Eunice Perrigo and he would continue to stare after her if it fell in with his purpose to do so, for he was as stubborn as the squire. He had been staring after Eunice since she was a little girl in short skirts instead of a young woman in shorter skirts—studying her, admiring this about her and deprecating that. She was a Perrigo, but unlike his father, he was capable of perceiving physical beauty even in one of that blood. She interested him, and sometimes she stirred his dry-rustling humor. What was to come of it? He asked himself that, and was rather of the opinion nothing could come of it, for Eunice had been raised to hate a Knuckles even as he had been raised to hate a Perrigo. One thing was clear—he did not hate her. He saw difficult times ahead of her, and that queer, rudimentary chivalry which one finds in his kind stirred uneasily within him.

If she were not a Perrigo he knew what he would do. He would have her—or know the reason why. Something about her, about her restlessness and recklessness, attracted him. He would have to marry, though there was no hurry about it, but he would be cautious about taking on that responsibility. One thing he knew, and that was that fear of his father's displeasure, terror of his father's curse, would not hold him back once he had made up his mind.

As to another matter he was perfectly clear; upon that nothing more was to be said, and from his determination no argument should move him: In what was to come—if anything was to come—Eunice should not be damaged if he could avert it. He had been brought up to know that the business of his life was to get back his own with ample interest and penalties from the Perrigos; but he did not hate as his father hated. He disliked and despised Walter, but had no sympathy with his father's root-and-branch belief. If the original wrong had been done to him, and not committed before his birth, he might have felt and acted as Eli did. But the offense was remote, one generation removed. And he had not his father's religion. . . . He walked down the steps, thrusting the Perrigos from his mind, for that day was to be devoted to a transaction. He had made up his mind to swap a tenement he owned next the post office for a farm with a good mowing and a wood lot situated on the edge of town. Also he fancied a penny might be picked up by renting Amos Pidgeon's sugar orchard for the coming year.

He opened his box in the post office, read his mail and sauntered out again upon the street. There he paused, leaning his shoulder against the building just under the big thermometer which advertised a brand of overalls, and studied the details of the transaction upon which he was about to enter. As he stood with eyes squinting, though, Eunice Perrigo drove up and stopped with a squealing of brakes and a dragging of rear wheels—a vehement, temperamental stop. Knuckles did not glance at her, and she passed within two feet of him with her nose a little in the air. She resented him, but, subconsciously, she resented his obvious and unstudied indifference.

Presently she came out again and got into her runabout. The starter ground, but the motor did not do its duty. She held her foot on the starter button viciously and jiggled the gas and spark levers. Nothing happened. Knuckles looked up.

"No good doin' that," he said, his shoulder still against the building. "Jest run out your batteries."

"Mind your business," Eunice snapped.

Imperturbably, exactly as if she had not spoken, or as if she were some person beside herself, he walked over to the car and lifted the hood.

"Leave that alone!" Eunice said in a flare of rage. "I don't want any help from you."

Knuckles raised his head and his eyes twinkled. "Then make b'lieve it's somebody else," he said, and ducked again into the machinery. In a moment he straightened up with a bit of the mechanism in his hand. "It's your points," he said. "Most always is on these cars. Got some sandpaper?"

"Put that down and leave my car alone!"

But he was scraping the points delicately with the blade of his knife until they shone clean to his taste; after this he replaced the housing and straightened up.

"She'll go now," he said.

"I'd rather have stood here all day!" Eunice said stormily.

"Matter of taste," said Knuckles. "You can still stand here, but the' hain't any need for it."

"If I were a man ——" Eunice said in a state of exasperation.

"Takin' all things into consideration," Knuckles said, "I cal'late it's full as fortunate you ain't."

Trembling with helpless rage, Eunice thrust her foot against the starting button much as if it had been Knuckles' face. The motor roared, she jerked into gear and hurtled recklessly across the square. Once again Knuckles stood and stared after her.

CHAPTER VIII

THE Perrigo house sat on a hilltop half a mile from the center of Colchester, and from its broad piazza one got such a view of mountain and valley and river as is seldom to be found even in regions of magnificent prospects. Even the natives admitted it to be sightly. It was a big house, preening itself upon that crest and patronizing the bowl in which the village lay. When it was erected by the father of Walter and James and Eunice the village resented it with some justice, recognizing the purpose of its owner to impress it with his wealth and his importance. He had not built it in that pleasant spirit in which a man usually makes himself a home, but boastfully, with intent to show his peers to what a height he had arisen; and he had tried to assume the attitude of lord of the manor.

Once each year it had been his custom to invite the village to a merrymaking upon his grounds—a condescending gesture to the peasantry. The peasantry came, trampled his grass, danced to his music, ate his ice cream and cake, but failed signally to pull its forelock; and when it went away again, it asked repeatedly the question, "Who in tunket does Amos Perrigo think he is?" It is difficult to found a local aristocracy with but one member.

Amos had amassed a fortune by various means and therefore was tendered a species of respect. A money-maker is always respected in that latitude where thrift is one of the cardinal virtues. But deference he never received, and it was one of his grievances against life that his contemporaries would not give over the habit of calling him Amos for the more respectful greeting of Mr. Perrigo.

Few people in that region are given the title of mister. The minister of the Gospel, of course—though the older-fashioned prefer to entitle him reverend—strangers who have not been admitted to the fellowship and visitors of note are spoken to by their family names. But all others, from eighteen to eighty, use the given name, as in the very nature of things it was intended to be used. A man who moves to Colchester and continues to be called Mr. Jones after six months of residence should pick out a new vicinage, for he will never succeed in this one.

So Amos Perrigo built his house and abrogated to himself importance in vain. Amos he was born and Amos he died. Nor did his children seek to carry on his tradition, though Walter showed sporadic signs of it in his earlier life. But Walter was astute; in his maturity he wore democracy as a well-fitting coat —but obviously tailored.

Strangely enough, in his will, Amos did not follow the law of primogeniture, as might have been expected. He did not leave the family seat to his eldest son; but, much to Walter's disgust, made it the property of his daughter. His property over and beyond that farm, with its mansion and its great, splendid barns and buildings, he divided into three equal parts, making Walter his executor and the guardian and trustee of his minor daughter.

But Walter, either with James' willing assent or by overriding his desires, continued as sole master of the property, managing it as his own and apparently accounting to nobody. Or, if he accounted to James, it was done privately, between themselves. At any rate Colchester came to look upon Walter as the man of wealth and his brother and sister in the light rather of son and daughter, who might inherit, but did not presently possess—which suited Walter to a nicety.

The three Perrigos sat at table, for it was one of those rare meals at which James was present, and held their peace while the servant was in the over-large room serving the dinner. But, as soon as the pantry door closed behind her, Eunice threw down her fork and turned furiously upon Walter.

"I shan't stand it any longer!" she said furiously. "Anybody would think I was a poor relative living on your charity."

James directed his attention upon his plate; if he heard the effect of Eunice's words it was not visible upon his tanned, expressionless face.

"Now what?" Walter asked provocatively.

"I'm sick and tired of coming to you for every cent I need. Anybody 'd think I was your wife."

"Lucky for you you aren't," said Walter.

"The money's mine, and I've a right to it."

"You've a right to what I give you."

"It's mine—mine as much as it's yours."

"It's mine—to take care of, and I'm going to take care of it. You throw away what I give you."

"And that's none of your business."

"It seems to be," Walter said in his most irritating tone.

"It won't be long," Eunice said furiously. "In ten months I'll be of age. . . . And right now I want an allowance—a decent allowance. I'm entitled to it."

"You won't get it," Walter said shortly.

"Won't I?" demanded Eunice.

"I think not."

"I'm not a complete fool."

"Not complete," Walter said.

"And I know my rights."

Walter laid down his knife and fork and leaned forward with sudden intentness.

"What are you talking about?" he demanded.

"My rights. And if you drive me too far I'll have them too."

"Who have you been talking to?"

"Never mind who I've been talking to."

"I won't have you running around blabbing family affairs."

"I'll do more than blab them. . . . I know, for

instance, that a guardian must file an annual accounting, and I know you haven't for two years."

Walter's eyes became curiously blank, his round bald head moved forward with the movement of an angered turkey cock.

"Who have you been talking to?" he demanded again, this time in a flat voice, with no syllable emphasized. The effect was menacing.

"It was about time I was finding out something. Now do I get a decent allowance or not?"

"You don't."

"You know," she said, and succeeded in making her voice maddeningly tantalizing, "I can have a next friend appointed by the court, and get an accounting, and ask the judge to order me an allowance —a suitable allowance, I believe is the word. Do you want me to do that?"

James looked up and spoke. "Oh, shut up," he said, his words directed impartially to both of them.

"I'll not shut up! And if you had a spark of decency in you, James, you'd help me out. You get what you want, don't you?"

"I don't want much," James said, and went back to his eating.

"I own this house," Eunice said.

"Who have you been talking to?" Walter demanded again.

"And you live all over it. You run it. You act as if it was yours."

"I want to know ——"

"Then find out," Eunice said, and then made a shot in the dark. "I'll bet you don't dare make an accounting," she said, "either to James or me. . . . I think now, and I've always thought, and I always will think, Walter, that you want it all—and you're trying to get it all somehow."

"Do you mean ——"

"I do. I think you're crooked. I think the mill people have found out you're crooked, and that's why they've sent Mr. Cross here. Why father ever trusted you ——"

Walter struck the table with his fist. "I want to know who's been putting this into your head, and I'm going to know."

"Go ahead and find out," Eunice jeered.

"I'll find out—and you'll tell me. Don't forget I'm running this place—and you too!"

"Guardian of the person and property," Eunice sneered. "Well, what do you think you can do about it?"

"I can stop your infernal tongue."

"You can—temporarily—by giving me an allowance. I'm not crazy about having our family rows gabbled about by everybody in the county. But that's the only way you can stop it—for ten months. Then you'll account, Walter, and I'll have a lawyer on the job to see you account right."

"I'll shut you in the house. If you're running around spreading stories ——"

James lifted his head again and looked frowningly from Eunice to Walter. "No," he said.

"Oh," Eunice said with curling lip, "so you won't let him lock me in my room, eh? That's nice of you, James. I wonder if maybe you aren't sort of afraid of the talk it would cause. Sometimes, James, I think you've a lot more brains than Walter. I've even had the idea Walter might be afraid of you."

James said nothing; Walter's eyes were baleful.

"Do I get my allowance?" Eunice demanded.

"No!" Walter shouted.

"Yes," James said quietly, without looking up.

"Don't you meddle with this," Walter said angrily.

James continued to eat. Walter sat back in his chair, his cheeks an unsightly gray, his breath audible.

"One thing or the other," Eunice said—"an allowance or dirty linen on the line."

"I'll ——" Walter commenced a threat, but did not utter it.

James interrupted. "How much?" he asked.

"For everything—my clothes and all I need—a hundred dollars a week."

"We can afford it," said James. "She gets it."

Walter pushed back his chair so that it crashed to the floor and stamped out of the room. Eunice sat still for an instant, surprised into silence. She had won where she had not expected to win, and with aid she had not anticipated to receive. More than that she was astonished at James, amazed that he should have asserted himself, and that, having asserted himself, he should so have dominated Walter. What did it mean? What was going on? Who, after all, was the actual head of the family?

In common with the rest of the world James had been a riddle to her. He had never opened his mind to her, as Walter had exhibited the contents of his mind. Walter was her natural enemy; they hated each other and made no pretense, in the privacy of their home, to conceal it. She never had been able to discover if James sided with her or with her brother, or if he were indifferent. Somehow his action today raised her suspicions. She concealed them.

"Thank you, James," she said.

He brushed aside her gratitude—perhaps recognizing it for what it was worth.

"Now keep your mouth shut," he said succinctly.

"Oh," she said ironically, "so I'm bought off, eh? You figured it was better to bribe me than take the consequences! Well, I'm bribed for ten months."

He got to his feet and stood over her, slender, dark, handsome, impenetrable, and looked down into her eyes calculatingly, with the scrutiny of a scientist studying a specimen. His eyes narrowed.

"Don't be a fool," he said.

With that he turned his back and left the room with that long, graceful, silent stride which always marked his progress. Eunice thought of leopards.

CHAPTER IX

WARREN CROSS, driving his car toward Colchester, picked up Knuckles and his rod and his fish basket, for Knuckles had been whipping the East Branch. The young New Yorker was rather glad of this opportunity, for though his acquaintance in the village was enlarging itself day by day, so that there were even some few men whom he called by their first names, he had got no closer to Knuckles than casual and passing speech. Knuckles was not approachable, as was Henry Bridge, for instance, or Larry Fox. There was a certain reserve and dignity about him, even when he walked about in his shirt sleeves; nor was Warren Cross one to make advances. He had been interested in Knuckles since that first view of him in the tavern, but Knuckles had not proffered his friendship; and Warren, who was at times both sensitive and self-conscious, had held back from making any advances.

This was different, however. He could do nothing else than stop his car to invite the plodding fisherman to ride, and Knuckles—even if he, as Warren sometimes in his self-conscious way thought, desired to avoid him—could not decline without deliberate rudeness. And your New Englander is seldom deliberately rude without an excellent reason. So he stopped his car and asked Knuckles to ride.

"Obliged," Knuckles said succinctly, and stepped into the car. They rode in silence for some minutes, Warren hesitating to open the conversation, Knuckles apparently seeing no need to do so.

"What luck?" Warren asked presently.

"Water's too low," said Knuckles.

Presently, as they turned a shoulder of the hill and came out upon an eminence giving a backward view of the valley and of the forested slopes of its gracious hills, Warren essayed a second attempt. "That looks," he said, with a wave of his hand, "like first-class timber."

"Ain't it?" Knuckles asked, biting off his words and seeming not to move his lips at all.

"I'm wondering." He laughed rather self-consciously. "About the only trees I saw until I came here were in Central Park. I've been an inside man. It seems as if I didn't know a darn thing about the things I ought to know about most."

Knuckles looked at him sidewise, but the expression of his face did not alter. "What's the matter with the timber?" he asked.

"That's just it. I've been thinking about having the office send up a competent cruiser to make an investigation."

"Cruised before they bought, didn't they?"

"Yes."

"Woods ain't changed much since," said Knuckles with a dry tone of finality.

Warren ventured to be direct. "You know this part of the country well. What is your opinion of our timber?"

"Some wind shake when you get up high."

"But in general?"

It seemed, however, that Knuckles was not to be driven into a downright opinion. He avoided. "What complaint you got against it?" he asked.

"Too much Number 3 Common."

"Much too much?"

"It runs more than 10 per cent over what I'd consider normal."

"What's James say?"

"Nothing." Warren did not want to tell Knuckles that it had been almost impossible for him to get an interview with James Perrigo and that when he had done so it was devoid of results.

"What's Walter say?"

"Walter says this and that, but it doesn't add up to anything satisfactory."

Knuckles made no rejoinder whatever to that. It was Warren's turn to eye his companion covertly. Knuckles' lean face was expressionless, the upper lip shut down upon the lower like the knife of a cutting machine. Cross thought he understood the young man's reticence; it sprang from that clannishness which he had heard was a characteristic of the people among whom he had come to live; it was a manifes-

tation of that passion for minding one's own business
which was regarded as among the highest virtues.
Knuckles would say nothing which might be con-
strued as a criticism of the Perrigos. And yet,
Warren reflected, there existed bitter enmity between
the Perrigos and Knuckles! As a matter of fact, he
did not understand at all. In the first place,
Knuckles was silent because of a congenital economy
of words; secondarily, he was silent because he was in-
tensely an individualist and desired to travel alone
and without allies the track he had marked out for
his feet to follow. Furthermore, he had not assayed
Warren Cross; had not appraised him so thoroughly
as to satisfy himself of Warren's quality. Innate
caution lay at the root of his silence.

"D'ye ever watch the saw?" Knuckles asked.

"I've watched it an hour at a time, and the logs going through seem of good quality."

"Sawyer ought to know about the run of logs,"
said Knuckles. "He's the one that bites into 'em."

"There's a certain hostility to me in the mill—perfectly natural, I suppose. The men don't talk freely
to me."

Knuckles' eyes flicked; it might have been a
twinkle.

"Once," he said very solemnly, indeed, "I, had a
man workin' for me. He was hostile." He paused
and pressed together his lips and his face grew even
more serious. "He went to work for somebody else."

People say your New Englander is without humor;

that his wit has been frozen out by hard winters. Such persons are ignorant; the New Englander method conceals the purpose—to those who do not know, and most especially to those not extraordinarily quick of perception. The New Englander does not shoot off his bon mots as if they were cannon; he is more subtle than that. When his dry wit crackles most brilliantly it does so to no accompaniment whatever, and he does not grimace to accentuate his point. Perhaps this is because he does not care whether you get his point; he has made it for his own private edification.

Now Warren was in doubt. He could not make out if Knuckles were stating uninterestingly a negligible fact, or if he spoke with intention and significance. If the latter, he recognized the excellence of the advice; but circumstances tied his hands so he could not follow it.

"I can't fire the whole shop," he said defensively.

Knuckles cleared his throat. "The jobs 'ud be there yet if you did, seems as though."

"Vacant jobs can't run a mill."

"I hired a man once to do a mean job of work. Didn't seem like anybody'd undertake it." Again that clearing of the throat. "He got through and the' was four men around in the mornin' after the place."

Warren launched on impulse a sudden attack. "Suppose," he said, "a job like running the woods end for me was open—would you take it?"

Only a prolonged silence hinted that Knuckles had been taken by surprise. "Don't seem like my hands 'ud fit around an ax helve James Perrigo just let go of," he said.

"There you are," said Warren.

Knuckles said nothing. Warren waited a moment; and then, driven by the necessity to put his thoughts into words—that necessity which sometimes compels all men—he said, "I want to be fair, Mr. Knuckles. I want that. I don't want to fire any men from jobs or remove any men from positions unless I am sure of my grounds. But something is wrong; something drastic must be done. I've been going slowly, feeling my way, but I've got to show results; I'm sent here to show results. If I don't somebody else will."

Knuckles said nothing; he was reflecting. If this man measured up he would bring matters to a crisis; if he were acute it would be some such crisis as Knuckles had been waiting and hoping for. But did he measure up and was he acute? The best way to determine that was to remain aloof and to watch. He liked Warren's looks, Warren's manners appealed to him, for there was nothing arrogant with city arrogance in it, nothing patronizing, and above all something modest and appealing. He did not pretend to know all that was to be known about the lumber business. Knuckles would wish him well, but not enlist under his banner. Outsiders had no part in the Knuckles-Perrigo feud—not directly. But Warren might prove an excellent unsuspecting ally.

"There's so much I can't understand," Warren was saying—"that a mill so profitable under the old ownership should suddenly become unprofitable, with the same management, under new ownership; that costs should have jumped and production dropped; that timber as reported by our cruisers should run to so much low-grade stuff."

"Did it use to?" Knuckles asked.

"No."

"Cuttin' off the same town, ain't you?"

"Yes."

"You'll be turnin' off here to the mill," Knuckles said with no change of tone as he abruptly changed the subject. "I'll get down and walk in."

"No, indeed. I'll drive you in. It won't take but a few minutes."

"Obliged," said Knuckles, "but I'll walk. . . . The's some difference between a man that thinks he's gettin' too much Number 3 Common and a man who knows he's gettin' too much of it. . . . Obliged for the ride. G'-by."

Warren stared after Knuckles a moment before he meshed his gears and took the turn toward the bridge. What did he mean by that parting shot? Warren was beginning to suspect that Knuckles meant something by everything he said, and used no words without a purpose. . . . Difference between a man who thinks and a man who knows. . . . It was cryptic. And didn't he, Warren Cross, know he was getting too much low-grade lumber, too much Num-

ber 3 Common, which is the bane of the life of the
lumberman, which clogs yards and is so slow of sale
as almost to be unsalable? Didn't his tally sheets
and inventories prove it to him? What did Knuckles
suggest?

He drove onward slowly, a line between his brows.
From Knuckles he had derived no information at all,
no direct answer to a question. But had he not derived something else? And if so, what? A meaning
had underlain Knuckles' speech, and Warren felt
that if he could puzzle his way to it he would be much
farther toward those results desired by him and his
employers than he was at present. Presently he left
his car under its shed, but instead of walking to the
office he stepped into the mill—into the vibration and
roar of belts and pulleys and shafting, the dull bunt-
ing thuds of the nigger as it placed with almost sen-
tient efficiency logs upon the carriage, the whine and
squeal of the saws as they ate their way into beech
and birch and maple. Men upon whose hats and
clothes and faces dust and sawdust lay thick moved
about him; chain conveyors carried from the band
saws to the horizontal resaws; streams of ashes
poured into the fireroom and slabs were tossed down
their chute to make fuel for the boilers. And the
odor of wet wood, of rotted bark, of fresh sawdust!
It was an odor new to him, but already he delighted
in it.

He stood upon the platform where men with cant
dogs rolled off the dogs of the hoisting chains logs

drawn up from the hot pond below, and watched the sawyer, who, with the saw filer in his busy attic high above, is the most skilled unit in an industry requiring skill and judgment on every hand.

Warren saw a huge log of red spruce bunted upon the carriage, saw the doggers and setters spring to their tasks of fastening it in place; saw the sawyer eye it and make a tentative cut, appraising the log, figuring in his mind's eye how to get from it the best results in board feet. He watched the carriage shoot back, saw finger signals pass, saw the nigger toss the log into the air, whirl it, catch it and adjust it exactly where and how the sawyer desired. He loved it; it fascinated him. For twenty minutes he watched, studying the run of the logs, and to him it seemed unusually fine. No overrun of Number 3 Common here —not today!

He followed the conveyors as they carried the boards in procession to the back of the mill, ready for grading and piling; and thence out into the yard, where narrow avenues ran off, it seemed almost into infinity, between tall leaning piles of boards white and yellow and red—beech, white maple, white and red birch. Then down the siding he walked, scrutinizing the piles, identifying with the unconscious knowledge of the specialist. . . . Number 3 Common! It was there, piles of it, avenues flanked with it—too much, far, far too much, in proportion to the richer, higher grades. . . . He did not think—he knew!

Fifty yards beyond, a car was loading, and he proceeded toward it, drawn by the interest of motion as men atop high piles passed boards down to men upon the car. Beside the tracks Warren stopped and watched. Here was no low-grade lumber, but great, wide, selected boards of finest red birch—birch fit for the piano factory, for the furniture dealer; fit almost to be classed with semiprecious and exotic woods from distant jungles; so fit, indeed, that, when polished and finished, the eye of an expert is required to tell you that your piano is not mahogany, as you suppose, or that your dining table is lowly birch.

"Nice stuff," he said to the checker, nodding with satisfaction.

"Fust-class, Mr. Cross."

"Who's getting this?"

"People's Lumber Company down to Boston."

Warren watched for a moment and then turned back toward the office, but as he went that line appeared between his brows. . . . People's Lumber Company! He recalled that order; it had come in a week before and had passed through his hands. He remembered glancing at it. He had been rather surprised, because the items had been a certain amount of dimension stuff and Number 3 Common. A satisfying amount of Number 3 Common—but he recalled no specification for red birch.

It seemed best to him to sit quietly in his private office for a little while, which he did, busying himself with the detail which had accumulated upon his desk.

Then he stepped to the filing cabinet in which were
the cards upon which were recorded the incoming orders. . . . P—People's Lumber Company.   He
withdrew and scanned the card. On it was no mention of selected red birch!

It might—it might be error; but just that sort of
error is difficult to make about a lumber mill. . . .
Suddenly he thought of Knuckles and that cryptic
saying about thinking and knowing. He went back
to his office and sat down before his desk, where he
called upon his reason to work for him in this emergency. . . . Too much Number 3 Common! Indeed! If red-birch selected were carried on the
inventory as Number 3 Common; or if it were ship-
ped out as Number 3 Common while the Number 3
was allowed to accumulate—then, with truth, there
would be too much of it!

Until that moment Warren had suspected incom-
petence, bungling, even willful extravagance and deliberate interference with efficient production. He
had been seeking for a way to defeat inefficiency and
ill nature, but never had he felt himself confronted
by overt dishonesty, by a plan not only to wreck the
mill as a profitable going concern but to rob it to
somebody's great financial advantage as well.

Either that car loading was a mistake, an impossible blunder, or there was conspiracy—conspiracy
shared by someone in authority within the mill and
by purchasers outside! Of a sudden he felt this discovery would not come as a surprise to Knuckles, and

as suddenly he put on his hat and strode out of the
office. His humor was savage and he did not trust
himself; he was afraid of taking ill-advised action
unless he left the place and the possibility of action
behind him for a time. . . . One thing he meant to
do—it could not be a misstep; at worst, it could do
no harm—he meant to take Knuckles into his confidence.

CHAPTER X

WALTER PERRIGO, round and bald and inconspicuous, looked up from his desk and frowned slightly.

"Well, Saxon?" he asked.

"That car's loaded. Papers ready to take up to the depot?"

"Here they are."

Saxon paused with the yellow sheets in his hand. "I dunno if any harm's done," he said, "but Cross seen it."

"Cross?"

"Yes, he was pokin' through the yard and stopped and watched us loadin' for a while. Wanted to know who the car was goin' to."

"Is that all he said?"

"Every word."

"All right, Saxon."

When the man was gone Walter sat quietly tapping on his desk with a pencil; he pursed his lips, and little wrinkles grew about his eyes so that suddenly they were transformed into the eyes of quite another person. No longer were they round and slightly staring; they were exceedingly sharp and capable. He got up presently and went into the outer office.

"Miss Biggs," he said, "Mr. Cross was just in, wasn't he?"

"Yes; he came in and went right out again."

"You didn't see him take last week's time sheet, did you?" Walter had no curiosity about last week's time sheet; he knew exactly where it was, but he had found indirection to be an efficient method, and one efficient to conceal his real purpose.

"No," said Miss Biggs. "He just came in here for a minute. Took a card out of the order files there and went back into his own room."

So Cross had come from the yards and had gone directly to the order files. It might mean nothing; it might mean everything. He went into his own room and inserted a card in his typewriter; on the card he entered an order from the People's Lumber Company for fifteen thousand feet selected red birch. Then from a locked and private drawer in his desk he extracted a letterhead—of the People's Lumber Company, of Boston, and wrote as follows:

"Supplementing our order of the 12th inst., ship at once 15 M red birch," and followed it with specifications. He signed it with the firm name in typescript, and then, with a blue pencil, scrawled an initial. To the letter he pinned the card, and watching for an opportunity when the bookkeeper was out of the room, slipped it in the wire basket on the standing desk. All this meant a distinct financial loss to himself and he did it regretfully. It might be he was taking a useless precaution, but Walter was not one to take chances. All that remained was to wait for Cross' return, when he would dramatize that supplemental order and effectively allay any suspicions which may have clouded Cross' mind.

But if it did not quiet suspicions—then what? It was Walter's custom to look on all sides of a question, and to peer into the future at all the possible results which might flow from any given action. It was a real pleasure to him to sit and think, to follow threads and to take out insurance against every possible contingency. He was not a man given to display of his powers; about him was nothing ostentatious. Indeed, he was at some pains to minimize himself and his astuteness—a course he had found invariably to be profitable. People do not take so many precautions in dealing with a dull man as with one reputed to be keen—and Walter preferred to be the one to take precautions.

One advantage he had at the outset, and this was that he knew exactly what he wanted. Remained then to plan the best, if not the quickest way to get it. And he was, strangely enough, a highly imaginative man, though not given to introspection. If he had a defect, and few men are without them, it was this: That he took himself for granted. Long hours he spent in the pleasant pastime of imagining what others would do if such-and-such a set of facts should group themselves, and in having on file the remedy. But he did not pursue his reflections to the ultimate; perhaps he dared not. Few of us like to reflect upon what we might be capable of if sufficiently driven by necessity.

For instance Walter's plans could not contemplate his removal from his present position. He had to be where he was, and there he must remain. The arrival of Warren Cross had not been altogether unexpected, but it had come sooner than he had anticipated. So far Cross had been troublesome, but not, so far as he could determine, dangerous. He undervalued Cross because of the latter's obvious lack of experience in the actual operating of a mill and in those complicated operations which transform a tree growing in a forest into a log lying on a pile in a mill yard. Just as Janet Cross looked with biased eye upon the people and activities of Colchester, so Walter looked with biased eye upon a man born and bred in New York City.

Suppose then Cross should stumble upon the real reason why costs in the woods were high, why production was low, why timber which should produce such-and-such results fell so far below expectations. In that case he would find himself suddenly removed from his place, with even more disastrous results to apprehend. It was inevitable he should realize that Cross regarded him with suspicion—not his honesty, indeed, but his efficiency. Very well, he must so contrive as to remain in place and to make Warren Cross appear inefficient as well; to make the mill, the whole enterprise, appear inefficient and unprofitable and not one desirable to be retained by a corporation such as the Consolidated Lumber Corporation.

His plans to that end were reasonably sound, barring accident—some such accident as had happened today. . . . What then if Cross should return to the mill and discharge him out of hand? He contemplated that. Having done so he gave some thought to his brother James and to his sister Eunice. They were all in it. He even thought of Knuckles and his father, the justice, and estimated what a satisfaction it would be to them if he should come a cropper. Then he made up his mind he must see James. By all means he must see James at once and take certain steps.

And then James came in. It was opportune, for even Walter could not always lay hands on James when he was wanted.

"You weren't at home last night," he said, without other greeting.

James nodded. "Till midnight," he said. "I got up and went out to Camp 6."

"I never did understand you," Walter said. "Why don't you settle down and be civilized? Getting up at midnight to tramp fifteen miles through the woods!"

"Better than sleeping," said James.

"But why? What's the idea of it?"

"You wouldn't understand if I told you."

Walter was silent at this, and James sank into a chair, from which he looked out of the window, across the yard, with its piles of lumber, to the lifting hills beyond. Walter studied him—almost Indian, he reflected. Handsome! But, after all, what was inside him? What was the fiber of this inscrutable brother of his? Was he anything but a forest runner?

"Where's Eunice?" he asked suddenly.

"How should I know?"

"Confound it! She's getting more highty-tighty every day."

"She doesn't like you," said James. "Maybe you've noticed it yourself." Walter could not tell if James were poking fun at him or if he were merely dull. Those quick roving eyes did not look dull. "She hasn't made up her mind about me," James went on. "But you, Walt—she doesn't trust you as far as a cat can spit."

"She isn't of age yet. One of these days I'll ——"

"What do you know about animals?" James demanded.

"What's that got to do with it?"

"You get to know a lot watching animals in the woods. You crowd her too far and she'll explode like a cornered bobcat. I've seen it in her eyes. She's fairly hated you since you sold this mill."

"Why doesn't she clear out—go to Europe or something?"

"Suggested it, have you?"

"I did."

James smiled—a peculiar, far-off, cryptic smile. "And right off that was the one thing she wouldn't do. You're no cat trainer, Walt. Now she knows you want her to go and nothing on earth will make her budge."

"Confound it! Why?"

"Because, Walt, she's watching you—and me."

"Eh?"

"Cat eyes," said James. "She knows you're up to something—and she more than half suspects I'm in it. Um—I sometimes wonder myself, Walt."

"Wonder what?"

"Oh, this and that. . . . And speaking of cat eyes, there's Cross."

"What about him?"

"Nothing much—except we're both going to be out of jobs one of these cloudy days."

"I've an idea," Walter said slowly, "that Cross'll be leaving here before I do."

"Don't agree," said James. "Unless he gets taken sick of a sudden—and it's a healthy climate."

"What are you getting at? What do you know?"

"Nothing," James said carelessly. "Only he's no fool. Personally I don't care. The woods'll be there, and I can walk in them whether I've a job or not. We've got money enough."

"We?"

"The three of us—you and Eunice and I." His eyes were not now the eyes of some creature of the forest, lovely to see and rather wistful. They were bland and expressionless—coal-black and remindful of those of an Indian chief in embassy at some alien council fire.

Neither spoke for some moments. Then James said: "He's getting pretty thick with Knuckles."

"Who?"

"Cross."

"Knuckles!" said Walter softly, and half closed his eyes. "Thick with Knuckles!"

"Thought it might interest you. Saw them driving together a while back—and not half an hour ago he stopped at Knuckles' house."

"A half hour ago!" Walter's eyes were almost closed now; he peered at his brother through narrow slits. "He went to Knuckles' house a half hour ago?"

"I saw him."

"Well, what of it?"

James lifted his shoulders. "I thought you might like to know," he said.

"What I'd really like to know," Walter said, and there was a disagreeable note in his voice, "is why you're hanging around that Cross girl?"

"Noticed it, did you?"

"The town's talking about it."

"Ever see her, Walter?"

"Naturally."

"Ever talk to her?"

"No."

"Just one more question on that subject: Walt, is it any of your darn business?"

"It might get to be."

"As how?"

"If you lost your head over her ———"

"Yes?"

"You might lose sight of which side your bread's buttered on."

"And then again," said James ironically, "Cross might hesitate to fire his brother-in-law—or otherwise, as the case might be."

Walter leaned forward. "What do you mean by that?"

"He mightn't be satisfied with just firing."

"Listen," Walter said, "I'm working for you as well as for me."

"Sure, for the Perrigo family—you and me and Eunice. . . . What if she should up and marry all of a sudden, Walt?"

"Not for ten months yet," said Walter grimly.

"Try to stop her if she takes it into her head!"

"Look here, Jim, you've been hedging and hinting around for an hour. Lay them on the table."

"Not today, Walt."

"You've got to do your share."

"Don't let that worry you. When the time comes for doing, I'll do." He paused and his eyes again looked far out of the window at the forested slopes of the hills. "I hate to think of anybody else owning that, Walt. It doesn't seem right."

"Nobody else will own it long—if we pull together."

"Maybe. . . . Well, I just dropped in to mention

that about Knuckles. . . . And if you don't want a cornered bobcat on your hands"—he lifted his shoulders expressively—"put some sugar in Eunice's feed box."

"Going?"

"Yes."

"Home to dinner?"

"Don't care for the atmosphere of meals in the Perrigo home. . . . No. Flat-rock fry out at the lake with the Bridges and Foxes and Crosses."

"That girl again, eh?"

"That girl again," said James, and went out with that graceful, soft-footed stride, that forward, panther-like sway of the shoulders. Walter stared after him—and again there was a deep line between his eyes.

CHAPTER XI

KNUCKLES was not at home when Warren Cross called; indeed, he was seldom at home. His place of business was the county. Unless one happened to run across him by chance, the only way to get an interview was to take up a station in front of the post office and wait until he turned up. If he wanted to see you he would find you; if you wanted to see him that was a very different matter.

Just now he was in the ice-cream parlor behind the grocery—where that confection was made from genuine cream—completing an important and somewhat intricate transaction in the realm of barter and trade. He had given considerable time and thought to this particular deal; it had consumed, in its various ramifications, the better part of a week, but at last it was being consummated—he was swapping a trombone.

The facts were these: Knuckles owned the trombone. At one time he had played it in the Colchester Silver Cornet Band. It was a first-class trombone, plated with silver and with a gold bell. But that musical organization had ceased to be some years before, and the instrument became merely an asset. Of course Knuckles might have attempted solos, but he did not; he merely put it away in its case and waited for the day when it would come into its own as something that somebody else wanted and would give good and valuable consideration to obtain.

That day had arrived with the formation of a new band, for bands came and went in Colchester. Every year or two there appeared a stranger whose avocation was leading brass bands. There are numbers of such individuals in this interesting world; men who must stand in the middle of the circle and stamp and wave with tremendous seriousness as they try to draw from eighteen or twenty assorted horns—to say nothing of the drums—the ever-popular strains of the National Emblem March. Such men are foreordained bandmasters; wherever they plant themselves for a year or a decade, the town hall will become terrible with brass. Generally they have whiskers, and in a surprising number of instances they are millwrights during the daytime.

Another surprising phenomenon is this: That any bandmaster arriving in a new town knows there is one instrument he will not have to worry about. He may have to teach the cornets and the altos and the drums, but there will be ready and waiting for him a tuba player. There is a tuba player in every village in America, awaiting eagerly the dawning of the day when a new band will organize. One does not easily perceive why some souls are in tune with this particular instrument, which seldom if ever accomplishes anything more intricate than to rumble the same umph-ah, umph-ah through each and every piece. But it is so.

That day had dawned in Colchester; the whiskered bandmaster had arrived, and of evenings one heard on all sides the not-soothing blare of cornets and altos and the somewhat hesitating *arpeggios* of the clarinet. So Knuckles' slide trombone was coming again into its own.

Willie Bassett coveted it and made advances. It was Willie who made and served the ice cream, and took a just pride in his accomplishment; but he could not do business with Knuckles. No; Knuckles would not sell for cash; that would involve too great a sacrifice from the original purchase price, and Willie owned nothing for which Knuckles would swap. But —and here the transaction commences to take shape —Luke Weaver owned a fine double-barreled shotgun which Knuckles desired. However, Luke was not interested in slide trombones. He was interested in a certain Holstein calf of more or less aristocracy. The owner of the Holstein calf had no desire either for trombone or shotgun, and there was impasse. However, he would sell for cash. And so, with infinite pains and diplomacy, Knuckles arranged it.

Willie Bassett, who wanted a trombone, bought for money a Holstein calf; then he swapped the calf for Weaver's shotgun; and now, in that back room, was swapping the lethal weapon for Knuckles' horn. The transaction had consumed more time and energy than many a bank merger, but Knuckles was content.

So long as he continued to own that superfluous horn he would have been uneasy. In the end, if this band-master had not appeared, Knuckles undoubtedly would have had to organize a band himself in order to create a market!

So, carrying his new gun, he crossed the street, to meet Henry Bridge, just coming from the bank.

"Hopin' I'd see you," said Henry. "Cross is all het up to see you. He was to your house."

"Say what he wanted?"

"No, but I told him I'd meet you, most likely. We're havin' a flat-rock fry out to the lake, and I told him I'd ask you to come. He wanted to see you bad."

"Um—who's goin'?"

"The Foxes and us and the Crosses and Eunice —and I guess maybe the Hewitts."

"Got everything?"

"Larry's tendin' to that—just drove down to get the steaks and things. Nice night for it, seems as though—and not many skeeters."

"Cal'late I can manage to come," said Knuckles. He knew he could manage to come, though it was not often he wasted his time on such affairs as flat-rock fries; those were for the young married folks and for such unmarried men as were engaged in the labor of courtship. His reason for accepting was not to see Warren Cross. He was not especially anxious to see Cross; and it was an axiom with him that if the other man were anxious to see him, he would be more anxious after a little delay. His real motive was Eunice Perrigo—and there was something of saturnine humor in it. He wanted to see how she would act in an intimate group of which he was a part.

He stopped for a moment in the squire's office, a dusty room containing a few wooden chairs and bookcases filled with reports of the Agricultural Department and of state commissions and such other volumes as had come gratis by mail during the last forty years. The sole lawbooks were the Compiled Statutes of Tiffany's Justice's Guide. On top of the bookcase were half a dozen astonishingly beautiful pewter tankards, tall, slender, graceful, ranging in size from a pint to a gallon. These were the ancient official standards of liquid measure of the township, and no collector had been allowed even to handle them.

"I won't be to supper tonight," he said.

The squire looked up from a conveyance he was drafting. "Where goin'?"

"Flat-rock fry out to the lake."

"Huh!" said the squire, and bent again over his document.

Knuckles left his newly acquired shotgun at home, pottered around for a time with the draw-shave out in the woodhouse, where in odd hours he was shaping an ax helve, and did considerable thinking. A great deal of it had to do with Eunice Perrigo, but it was not the sort of daydreaming usually indulged in by a young man in such circumstances. It was highly practical, involving not at all the color of Eunice's eyes and the slenderness of her ankles and the loveliness of her disposition—which did not strike him as extremely lovely—but rather with her relations with Walter and James and the probable outcome of their involved family affairs.

He did not give a great deal of time to Walter, who was a known quantity to him; but James—so much revolved about James, about the basic character of James, which nobody had solved; about James' relations with Walter and how far he was tarred with Walter's brush; about the question as to whether James were not after all the directing mind in the affair. He felt that James could be just that. On the other hand James might be completely bamboozled by the devious Walter and so not to be considered at all. Here lay the weakness of the position. It was impossible to move until he found the answer to James—and it was not printed in the back of the book.

He also reflected upon Warren Cross and estimated his potentialities. Warren had yet to prove himself, though it was certain that the mere coming of Cross into the picture was urging affairs to some climax. . . . And Cross wanted badly to see him. That meant something had happened, but Knuckles could not imagine what.

"Let him chop his own stove wood," was Knuckles' conclusion.

Presently he washed his hands, trundled his car with the flapping mud guards out of the barn, and drove somewhat jumpily toward the lake. The car had been acquired in a trade and it sufficed. So long as it continued to move from place to place without giving too much trouble it would continue to suffice, for Knuckles worried little about appearances. Some engine trouble was welcome; it gave variety to the journey, for he loved to tinker.

Up the pleasant valley he drove, across the meadows and the brook which meandered there quietly between grass-grown banks and harbored in its shadows speckled trout. Twenty minutes later he turned to the left into the woods and drove over granite outcrop at great hazard to springs until the road dipped and ran muddily through never-diminishing shade. Other cars had passed that way, and he followed in their ruts. In a little while he came to an upland, dry and stripped of growth; and then, dipping sharply past a dilapidated boathouse, he drove out upon the tongue of land where it was the custom to picnic in a little stand of spruce.

Larry and Edna Fox were there, and Kitty Bridge. Henry was collecting firewood.

"The old rock's split," Larry said. "Got a new one located—just waitin' for some more beef to help get it down. Here's Hank. Come on, we'll fetch it in that dray of yours."

They clambered in and drove back up the hillside, where they lifted a rock, some six inches thick and about a yard square, into the tonneau. By the time they returned the Cross family had arrived, Sarah with James Perrigo, and Eunice alone in her blue runabout. Then the Hewitts came—a little later on account of the baby.

"I do hope you got the meat up where bugs can't crawl over it," Amanda said with her first breath, after she had labored out of the car. "The last time ——"

"Don't you worry, Mandy; we'll de-bug it," said Henry Bridge, glancing at Janet Cross to see how she took it. None of them were yet fully at ease with Janet, nor was Janet with them. Just now she was exceptionally uncomfortable, warm and a bit sticky, with a feeling that invisible insects crawled over her itchily. She had experienced picnics on the beach, with the surf breaking and civilized folks in bathing suits on all sides, but this was too primeval for her. . . . Sarah pried a nugget of spruce gum off a tree and chewed it with relish. "Should have had this fire going an hour ago," complained Larry; "it'll take forever to heat this rock."

The men set the rock and built a blaze over it; then they heaped wood over it, so that presently it was concealed by fire which crackled and sent its smoke just where it was least desired. Janet coughed and moved away. While it was heating Tom Hewitt organized a game of duck on a rock, which everybody, men and women alike, played except Janet and Mrs. Hewitt. Sarah enjoyed the boisterousness of it, and Eunice pitched her rock with a sort of vindictive efficiency. She resented Knuckles' presence; he, on his part, ignored her utterly. James flitted about darkly in the background, his eyes seldom forsaking Sarah.

"Heavens!" whispered Janet, as Warren sank down at her side when the game broke up through the sheer exhaustion of the players. "Is this what they call amusing themselves?"

"Hush! I don't know when I've had more fun," he said.

"You need a bath. . . . I never shall be able to eat a bite in all this dirt. . . . What they see in it ——"

But now Larry was scraping the fire off the top of the rock. He swept it carefully with a whisk broom and covered it with white slices of salt pork. These began to sizzle and curl and diminish in size as they took on a golden-brown color, and the top of the stone bubbled with grease. Next he heaped on what seemed like half a bushel of sliced onions, which frizzled in the grease and gave off an odor not reminiscent of the Ritz, but nevertheless curiously appetizing. Janet began to be conscious of appetite.

Presently the onions were raked aside, and the rock covered with thick steaks and broilers halved. Then the onions were heaped over them again, and Janet began to think possibly she could eat a morsel dirt and all. A pail of coffee was making over a separate fire and corn was boiling in a kettle. The conversation was not edifying to one whose thoughts were on higher things, and perhaps were not carefully chosen.

"I could eat a raw dog with his tail on," Henry said with unction, and Janet shuddered.

"Never tried any dog," said Larry, "but I could raise thunder with a dead owl."

And this, thought Janet, was what passed for humor in these parts!

When everything was done Henry and Larry served—in their shirt sleeves, with grime mixing on their perspiring faces. You could see they were proud of their achievement. Henry brought Janet a wooden plate so full of food it offended her—but the odor of it could offend nobody.

"Wait a minute," Henry said, anxious to please, "and I'll kind of slosh a hunk of bread around in the juice for you."

"Never mind, thank you."

She dropped her fork. Henry picked it up, wiped it on his sleeve and handed it back to her; but he did not, fortunately, see the look in her eyes. It was not one of gratitude. "If you sit kind of in the edge of the smoke, the skeeters won't bother you," he said solicitously. "Just a minute and I'll get you coffee. Then I'm comin' back and we'll make an evening of it together. I bet your husband'll be wanting to lick me before we start home."

Janet looked about for Warren, but he had withdrawn a little way and was eating with Knuckles;

their faces were serious and she sensed business, so she did not summon him to her side.

"Mr. Knuckles," Warren was saying in a cautious tone, "I tried to see you this afternoon. . . . Seriously, will you consider taking on the woods job?" Knuckles was silent. "I've got to clean the Perrigos out. I hate to do it. It will make things difficult, but I've got to."

"Why?"

"I've found out why we run to Number 3 Common." His jaw set determinedly. "Found we were shipping out a car of selected red birch this afternoon on an order for Number 3. I wasn't looking for downright crookedness."

"Want I should run the woods, eh? Why?"

"I need a competent man, and one I can rely on."

"But," said Knuckles, "James don't run the shipments."

That was true. James had nothing to do with shipments, nor with buying supplies; indeed, he was concerned only with cutting and delivering logs.

"If one is in it, both are," said Warren.

"That ain't proved," said Knuckles. "Mebby there was some mistake."

"No; I checked up."

"It's none of my business," Knuckles said.

"I'm trying to make it your business. Somehow I've a feeling it is your business."

Knuckles peered at Warren. This man was no fool; he could see through a grindstone if there was a hole in it! And his back was up. Knuckles was conscious that his hand was being forced, that he would have to come in before Warren snarled things up. He was not ready yet for a forced issue, and to discharge the Perrigos certainly would bring matters to a premature climax.

"James is watchin' us," he said.

"Let him watch."

"I don't know about James," Knuckles said. "If I was you I wouldn't jump till I could see what I was landin' on. Walter's a rotten egg, but I ain't sure about James. . . . No, I won't take that woods job—not yet."

"Why?"

"There's more in this than shipping the wrong lumber," said Knuckles.

"What do you know?"

"Walter's a hog," said Knuckles. "He's not after what he can make with a little crookedness. . . . There's no love between us Knuckleses and the Perrigos."

"I know."

"If I only knew where James stood."

"No one seems to understand James."

"Your sister seems to be in a fair way," said Knuckles. "And there's Eunice."

"What about her? She can't be mixed up in it."

"Walter's turned the whole estate into money, hasn't he? All but the big house and the farms there?"

"Yes."

"Ever wonder why? Where would he put his money to do better than in the mill?"

"I've wondered about that."

"There was three owned the mill," said Knuckles.

"And three own the money."

"But," said Knuckles, "money's easier to juggle than a mill."

"You mean ——"

"Walt wants it all—or he and James want it all. And then he cal'lates to buy back the mill—cheap. Your company's kind of sick of its bargain, isn't it?"

"You mean he'd work some skulduggery on his own sister?"

"If," said Knuckles, "Walt could sneak his fingers into his own pants pocket and get 'em out without catching himself at it, he'd steal his own wallet."

"Will you work with me?"

"No," said Knuckles dryly; "but you can work with me. I been on the job some years. . . . The Knuckles family wants its own back. And there's Eunice."

"Don't you include her in the feud with the Perrigos?"

"It kind of looks," said Knuckles, "like I was makin' a special case of her."

"You don't think it best to fire the Perrigos?"

"Not yet. . . . I'm wondering how far Walt can force himself to go. If I was sure about James I'd know what's being risked. If James is in it he'll stop nowhere. But Walt ain't what you'd call darin'."

"Just what are you getting at?"

"I mean," Knuckles said, "that maybe if Walt finds it kind of hard to grab all the estate he might figger to inherit it."

"That's a mighty serious thing to say."

"It's a mighty disturbin' thing to think, and is why I want you should go slow. . . . James is eyin' us. We've talked enough."

He got up presently, walked over to refill his coffee cup and did not rejoin Warren. Warren, startled, disturbed as he had never been before, watched James with fascinated eyes. . . . James and his sister Sarah!

CHAPTER XII

JANET CROSS tolerated Henry Bridge much as she might have tolerated the amiabilities of her butcher during negotiations for the Sunday roast. Of course there was a difference, for Henry was a banker—and even a country banker is more eligible than a city tradesman—but it was slight. She considered such manners as he had to be free and jovial, and set herself to look for crudities even where no glaring crudities existed. But she could not repel the effect of his kindliness, his ebullient good humor and his evident desire to amuse. Nor could she repel utterly the attacks made upon her disapproval of the whole evening by the toothsomeness of that steak and broiler.

With the lifting of the moon over the saucer walls of mountain which contained the lake, a breeze, refreshing, cooling, tonic, sprang up and brought an end to the mosquitoes. She found herself being comfortable, and without question there was beauty to charm.

A dozen feet away, Larry Fox and Tom Hewitt and fat Amanda Hewitt—with the intriguingly beautiful speaking voice—and Kitty Bridge were organizing themselves into an impromptu quartet to sing My Bonnie Lies Over the Ocean. James Perrigo sat with his back against a tree, his lean, striking face defined by the moonlight, and seemed to watch rather than to talk to Sarah. And then Henry Bridge, that rather vulgar young man, commenced to talk to her, not with boisterous humor, not with clumsy clowning, but in a simple and straightforward sort of way—somehow the whole proceeding seemed less absurd and bucolic.

"Mrs. Cross," said Henry, "you're kind of uncomfortable here. A body with half an eye can see it. Just like any of us would be uncomfortable in New York. We're all different from your friends, and we have to like different things, because up here we kind of have to make our own fun if we have any. I dunno but what it's as good a way as the other, but then I'm used to it and all. But what I wanted to say to you, Mrs. Cross, is we're all awful glad to have you here, and we want you to like us." He paused, embarrassed and awkward.

Janet looked down at him as he sprawled, coatless, beside her. She was conscious of a little feeling of shame—ashamed because she was self-accused of snobbery. And he was so sincere and so kindly. Suddenly he became more tolerable to her, though no gentleman as she knew them would have said just what he had said in the way he said it.

"Why," she said—and there was a little gasp of surprise and of feeling in her voice—"why, thank you, Mr. Bridge."

"I just wanted you to know," he said; and then,

in embarrassment, blew his nose very loudly. And he had to make a joke to cover his confusion: "One advantage is, the' ain't any cover charge to a flat-rock fry."

Warren Cross found himself with Eunice Perrigo on his hands. He did not know just how it had come about and did not like it. The situation was disturbing; more disturbing as he glanced uneasily across at James and his sister. He would have to warn Sarah to go easy with that young man. Eunice interrupted his unpleasant reflections.

"Lots of times," she said in her pert way, "people talk to each other."

"I'm sure I beg your pardon," Warren said. "I ——"

"—— was looking with a hard cold eye at James Perrigo," she finished for him.

"Eh? . . . Not at all."

"Don't be silly. Everybody knows all the Perrigos hate each other. If I had to be shut up in an office all day with Walter I'd kill him. The best thing about James is that you never see him. . . . When are you going to fire my brothers? Everybody's waiting for it. You know—like the man who wouldn't throw down the other shoe."

This was disconcerting; he was not equipped to meet such nonplusing frankness.

"That steak was wonderful."

"—— said he, abruptly changing the subject." Eunice laughed, but there was something slightly acid in the tinkle of it. "It'll serve Walter right if you fire him. He had no business selling the mill. That's a Perrigo mill."

"But, really, I had nothing to do with buying it."

"Of course not. . . . I like your sister and Mrs. Cross. I hope nothing happens to take Sarah away." She paused. "Some day I'm going to tear out of this place myself and burst with a loud, reverberating bang some place where it will be a satisfaction to blow up. . . . In ten months ——"

"What—in ten months?"

"I'll be of age. Then you'll hear something—if it doesn't come before. I'm about fed up on Perrigos, and the Lord knows if I can live through another year of them! . . . What's Ab Knuckles doing here? Nobody ever invites him places I'm going. Everybody knows I despise the sight of him."

"You're a frank young person," said Warren.

"Oh, he despises me just as much. It sort of adds a zest to life, despising back and forth like that. . . . I understand my father did some kind of a dirty trick to Knuckles' father. I don't know just what, but if it was a Perrigo trick it was probably pretty raw."

Warren chuckled. He couldn't help it. Such appalling frankness in matters which any normal person would have avoided even in conversation with intimates did become humorous after a while.

"Well," he asked, "why don't you marry and leave your family on its uppers?"

"Marry who?" she said scornfully. "There isn't a young man in town would marry me on a bet. They're all afraid of me. I bite! And if there were I'd have to cut out his tongue and put in phonograph records of my own choosing. . . . It's too bad you're married."

Warren laughed again. "Would you have a try at me?" he asked.

"I'm not sure I shan't anyhow. After all I might as well be a full-blown Perrigo. Are you susceptible?"

"Not very. I'm a stodgy old gentleman."

"Most men are stodgy, when they're not worse. I don't know that I'd object to a little stodginess. . . . Now there's James. I've never been able to make up my mind about James—whether I hate him worse than I do Walter, or what? He's a something-or-other, James is. But if he didn't happen to be my brother, and I wasn't more or less obligated to dislike him, I could marry him."

"Most people seem to reserve their decision on James."

"Anyhow he isn't stodgy. And he looks as if he could make family life exciting."

"Is that your ideal of marriage?"

"Yes; and I'll get it too. If my husband doesn't make it exciting for me I'll make it darn exciting for him. . . . I never saw James all snarled up over a girl before—and a city girl at that. She might as well marry something out of the zoo." She paused and considered the situation. "Either James is two-thirds wild animal—or he just acts like one to keep out of the mess at home."

Warren looked again and more uneasily at Sarah and the puzzling young man.

"He'd probably make her live up in a tree," said Eunice reflectively. "Can you imagine it? I can't exactly see her hanging from a limb, can you?"

The conception tickled Warren, even though it disturbed him. The notion of Sarah and her lip stick and her jazz and her later-than-the-latest fashions keeping house in a tree top and shopping for beechnuts among the fallen leaves was too much of a contrast not to provoke a smile.

Eunice got to her feet. "Well," she said, "I've sat in one spot about as long as I can stand it. I'm going to get myself disliked." She crossed to James and Sarah and sat down with impish determination. "Hang out the welcome sign," she said. "You might as well." James eyed her darkly.

As for Knuckles, he prowled. Having satisfied his appetite he walked over to the old boathouse—in which he had no interest either financial or sentimental—and tinkered with the door. It was in disrepair and sagged from its top hinges. Knuckles braced it up, plugged the ancient screw holes, and with the driver blade of his enormous jackknife put in the screws again. Probably none would ever make use of that boathouse, which he knew perfectly well, but anyhow the door would open and shut. He repaired

it because he could not help it. Having set his mind
at ease in this respect he prowled back again toward
the fire and sat down close to the singing group. He
did not sing, neither did he interrupt with conversation—he sat. Presently he got up again and
prowled until he had found a rusty tin dish with a
handle; this he brought over and left beside the fire.

During the whole evening he had not approached
Eunice Perrigo, and if he had so much as looked at
her, none had detected it. But he was aware of her
constantly, unconscious of her presence as he might
have seemed. He listened to her voice—a very distinct and pleasant voice; he considered what she said
and stored it away in his mind. It was a satisfaction
to him that no individual in Colchester except his
father guessed that his interest in Eunice was acute.

She disliked him, he knew—and did not trouble
his head about it. It was an inherited dislike, a family dislike. As for himself she knew him not at all.
When the time was propitious he would find means
to disclose himself to her more fully and to abate
her aversion. There is no question that he was
embarked upon a courtship, that he was fully aware
of it and that he had studied the matter from all
sides. A Knuckles courting a Perrigo! It would
tickle Walter almost to death! Indeed, it tickled
Knuckles.

The hour advanced and the air grew chilly; restlessness manifested itself, until finally Amanda Hewitt announced that she must get home to relieve the

girl who was staying with her baby. Knuckles took
the tin vessel which his forehandedness had provided
for the purpose and doused the fire with water from
the lake. Couples got up creakily and climbed into
their cars; Eunice lashed off alone in her blue runabout; everybody else chugged away—and then
finally Knuckles, in his dilapidated machine.

Eunice was at the main road before the others
turned off the finger of land on which the fry had
been held; good roads or bad roads made no difference to her impetuosity. If springs were broken
someone else would have to mend them. At the edge
of town she turned off on the side road which led
to the house her father had built, and which was
her own property by his last will and testament. Her
lights shone on the figure of a man walking toward
her. It was her brother Walter, and as she flashed
by him without speaking, and rather regretting there
was no puddle with which she could splash him, she
wondered where he was going at that time of night.
Walter was usually to be found in his bed after ten,
and on most nights in the house after dinner. Here
it was half-past ten, and Walter was going out!

She ran her car into the garage, stopping it by
a miracle when it seemed she must crash it through
the back wall, swung her feet over the door and without opening it leaped to the ground. The house was
dark. It bulked huge and black against the moon,
but Eunice liked it even then. It was hers. In ten
months it would be hers with no restraining strings,

no guardianship to irk. And she would have plenty of money to run it. She stopped to regard it affectionately. Well, when it was hers it should be hers, and nobody should meddle with her in her management of it. It would cause a neat little scandal in Colchester, she knew, but she was resolved that on the day of her majority she would commence to live in it alone. At any rate Walter should get out of it! Her dish was full of Walter!

Some girls would be timid about entering a huge dark house, but not Eunice. She did not give that matter a thought, nor that the pair of servants were sound asleep in a wing distant from her bedroom. The back door was unlocked, as was the front. People in Colchester did not commonly know where were the keys to their houses, and there were doors in the village which had never been locked. Against what would one lock a door? . . . She entered the kitchen and felt about for a lamp. No electricity, of course, at that advanced hour of the night—almost eleven! Excepting when someone gave a party and paid especially for the service, power was turned off at 10:30.

Carrying the lamp before her she traversed the pantry and the dining room and the hall. The broad stairs confronted her, lifting out of the yellow light of the lamp into impenetrable blackness. Eunice did not notice the blackness, but mounted the stairs as quickly and as jauntily as a wabbling lamp chimney would permit. . . . One thing she would have when

the house was hers—one of those lighting plants she
had read about in the advertisements.

She went into her own room and closed the door.
It was a large room, and comfortable, with furniture
which she had selected herself and cretonne hangings
of blazing design. . . . It takes the modern young
lady a very short time to undress—one gets the impression they might do it with one energetic wriggle.

"I'm glad I've got pretty legs," she said to herself. "It's a good idea to have pretty legs."

She thrust them into silk pajamas—one of the
very few suits owned in Colchester either by men or
women—and sat on the edge of the bed, holding an
excellent foot in one hand as she crossed one leg over
the other knee. It was a satisfying picture, even
though her face was bent in a frown. She was thinking about Knuckles, who had so successfully ignored
her all the evening, and finding notable pleasure in
estimating just how much she disliked him. Then
she cocked her head to listen; it seemed to her a car
had driven up to the house. She went to the window
and looked out to see if James were returning. But
no car was in front; and, anyhow, James ought not
to be coming back so soon from the Crosses'. Again
she cocked her ear, and lifting the lamp went out
into the hall and across to Walter's room, which gave
upon the driveway and the garage.

It was not that she was especially curious, but she
was restless and not at all sleepy, and it gave her
something to do. Eunice always welcomed something

to do. She went to Walter's window and looked out. No car was there. With a thought that she must have imagined it she turned away, and then peered curiously about Walter's room. She could not remember when she had been in it before. There was his bed—that was where Walter slept. She made a little face at it, letting it suffer vicariously in Walter's absence. His dresser was old-maidishly neat, and the room had a sort of clothespress odor as if Walter slept with his windows closed. He would, she thought. It would be just like him.

Then she noticed a box against the wall—something like a small steamer trunk, but not of the wardrobe variety. When had Walter got that, and what for? She could not remember it as among his possessions. Still he could have a million things without her knowing or caring. Having nothing else to do she stood and stared at the box and wondered about it. A bunch of keys dangled from the lock—which signified two things: First, that Walter considered it worth while to keep it locked and second, that for once in his meticulous life he had been careless. The temptation was too great to resist. Really she hoped the box would contain something discreditable to Walter, in which case she could save up her knowledge to gibe him with in some hour when a gibe would come in handy.

So she knelt and turned the key and lifted the top. The box, or trunk, was not full. It was little more than half full—but it did not contain clothing.

It contained nothing one would have expected to find there. Indeed, its contents startled Eunice so that she turned quickly, big-eyed, to stare about her. In some queer way it made her feel afraid, her who was never afraid of anything. For the contents of the box was money—bills in neat packages, with narrow belts around them as they had come from some bank. Nor were they small bills; hundreds and fifties! She lifted a package and pinched it to make sure of its reality—fifty one-hundred-dollar bills. That was five thousand dollars—and there were dozens of such packages. Never before had she seen such a sum of money. There must be—she drew her breath as she estimated—why, there must be at least a hundred thousand dollars!

Softly she closed the cover and locked it, allowing the keys to dangle as she had found them. Then, very softly and with infinite caution, she tiptoed to the door. Somehow she had a feeling it would be unpleasant to be seen there—by Walter. At the door she listened and peered down the hall. Reassured she crossed it swiftly and closed her own door behind her and put out the light, even before she got into bed. But she did not lie down; instead, she sat with knees under chin, clasping her ankles, and pondered this phenomenon. And always she returned to one question: What was Walter doing with it?

CHAPTER XIII

IT WAS at breakfast next morning that Warren Cross, well knowing he was deliberately backing up to trouble, ventured to give advice to Sarah. "Sis," he said, "if I were you I'd step on the soft pedal with James Perrigo."

Sarah divorced her attention from the excellent pancakes and the superb maple sirup to stare at her brother. He was acquainted with that stare; whenever it focused itself upon him he became aware of the helplessness of the male animal in its dealings with its womenfolks. All women stared like that, he had discovered. Janet did it; other men's wives did it. There was something of outrage in the stare, something of infinite stubbornness, something peculiarly irritating in its challenge. He wished he had kept his mouth shut and let matters go, for he was about to be put in an absurd position. For any man can issue an ultimatum to the women of his household, but how can he enforce it? There is something grinding and humiliating to a man when he knows he is right, knows he is acting for the best of all concerned, and, venturing to assert himself, is told by word or action that he will not be heeded, and what, if anything, is he going to do about it? Well, what can he do about it? Gone are the good old days of the English common law which permitted a man to chastise with a club if not greater than the bigness of his thumb.

"No!" said Sarah with elaborate sarcasm. "And why should I put on the soft pedal with James? Is he a naughty boy, or has he something catching?"

"I'm advising you for your own good," he said, falling into that ancient error and delivering himself into the hands of the enemy.

"What you think is my good, or what I think is my good?" she asked. "Be your own sweet self, Ren, and go out in the yard and practice minding your own business. There are records for it on the phonograph, with appropriate exercises."

"But," Janet interjected, "what's wrong with Mr. Perrigo?"

"Wrong!" said Sarah, and giggled exasperatingly. "Can't you see for yourself, Janet? He's left-handed."

Warren pushed back his chair and withdrew, not quietly but with what he hoped was an air of hurt dignity. His disposition was not at its best, for he had slept little. The discovery of the day before had been on his mind, and Knuckles' advice to delay action. If it had been his own mill, if he had not been the employee of others and trusted by them, it would have been different. He could then have exercised his own discretion in the matter; but he felt he could not, in fairness, do so now. The Consolidated was interested in the success and welfare of the mill only; extraneous matters and individuals did not concern them. He had not been sent to Colchester to involve himself and the company in the concerns of the Perrigo family, no matter how dark and devious they might be. His duty was to act for those who paid him his salary. On the other hand he had gone to Knuckles and asked his advice.

He drove to the mill and went frowning to his desk. There, the first thing to come under his eye was the supplemental order from the People's Lumber Company pinned to the record card. Had he, then, been wrong? He held letter and card in his hand and studied them. Perhaps it would be better to wait, in view of this; to wait until he could take an inventory of the stock in the yard to determine if it tallied with the stock sheets. Then, of a sudden, he slammed the papers down upon his desk and pressed a button.

"Ask Mr. Walter Perrigo if he will be so good as to step in here," he said to the young lady who appeared.

Walter came, not on the heels of the order, but after sufficient delay to save his face. It was the first direct order he had received from Cross, the first time he had been required to present himself as a subordinate.

"You wanted to see me?" he asked casually, his round face bland and expressionless.

"Come in," said Warren, "and shut the door."

Walter did so, but remained standing. "When," asked Warren, "did this order come in?"

"The day before yesterday, I believe."

"In the usual course—by mail?"

"How else would it come?"

"Yes, how else? I noticed that car loading yesterday afternoon. But neither this order nor the card was in the files."

"Mislaid, probably," said Walter.

"Apparently. . . . Mr. Perrigo, as you know, I was sent here because things were going wrong. It is my job to find why they are going wrong and to take steps to remedy the condition. As an experienced millman you know the situation as well as I —probably better."

"It's been a bad year," said Walter.

"But," said Warren, "it's going to be a better year, beginning now. I've decided, since looking over this order, that this mill will benefit by the elimination of a good deal of Perrigo. For instance I am certain no one else could have an interest in shipping high-priced birch on an order for Number 3 Common."

"You are making a charge," Walter said in his quiet voice. His eyes lost their roundness, became steely and motionless.

"Why, yes—which I shall follow up to a conclusion. There is, of course, conspiracy between yourself and this People's Lumber Company. I would have put up with incompetency as long as I could, but downright crookedness is something else. In the language of the village, you are getting through, Mr. Perrigo. In fact, you are all through now."

"If I were you, Cross, I'd be careful. You can't run around making charges against me—unless you've got something a jury will take as proof."

"Perrigo," said Warren, "it's fortunate for decent folks that the crooks aren't infallible. . . . So this order came in the day before yesterday—by mail?"

"I've told you so."

"You didn't happen to save the envelope, did you?"

"Of course not."

"Because I should like to see it. It must be a peculiar envelope for a business house to use. . . . It was reported to you that I saw that car loading, and probably that I came in to examine the files. So you got busy without a moment's delay. But it pays to be more deliberate. . . . I've read in detective stories that all typewriters differ just as handwriting differs. I've an idea we can find one in the office that typed this order. . . . But the main thing, Perrigo, is something else again. It's hard to see how this letter came by mail, in an envelope, without being folded. I'm not setting up as a detective, and I don't claim to be amazingly bright, but I did notice that after a while. . . . Now I'm telling you to get your hat and put it on carefully and get off the place at a rapid walk."

Walter rubbed his hand across his mouth, stood

regarding Warren while the clock ticked half a dozen times; and then, turning abruptly on his heel, went softly out of the office. Warren watched him cross the outer room to his own place, take his hat off the hook and walk to the door. Cross was conscious of a little surprise that the man did not delay to collect his personal belongings.

Again he pressed the buzzer. "Have word sent to Mr. James Perrigo that I want to see him at once," he said. Now that he had started he was going to make a clean sweep of it.

Perhaps a quarter of an hour later the girl stepped to his door. "They want you over in the log yard," she said.

"Who does, and what for?"

"They didn't say."

He was glad to go, whatever it was; any minor emergency was welcome to take his mind off that unpleasant interview. He went out through the mill, winding his way among conveyors and resaws and rushing belts; past the saw carriage as it rushed back and forth shuttle-like, and down the soggy stairway leading to the concrete-walled hot pond. Here he paused a moment to watch the cables snaking logs across the river from the yard beyond, where they were stored in mountainous piles. There was something inexorable about that cableway as it squealed and grunted and tugged; something satisfying as it dragged its chainful of logs, bumping and rumbling down from the top of a great pile, across the intervening bark and mud, to surge through the muddied water to the higher shore.

It was not Broadway, but, in its way, it was more dynamic and purposeful than Broadway. He liked it. In New York there was struggle, battle, restless enterprise, amazing industry; but it was man against man, human being competing with human being. There it was—or so it seemed to him—only that part of man which lay indirectly under his hat which came into play.

But here the struggle was with the inanimate, against a product of Nature, against impediment placed in the way by mountain and river and storm. He was at the source, one of the sources, of that wealth which played its fountains in New York. Without this mill and other mills, without mines and forests and oceans and farms—unless men sweated and bruised themselves, unless muscles bulged and feet trampled, and perils were dared and overcome in such places as this, there could be no New York. The wealth was here; it was only dealt in there as a commodity. He was astonished at himself as he stood there reflecting—astonished to find that already this was getting into his blood, and that he liked it!

He traversed the pond and crossed the bridge. The warm damp odor of water-soaked bark was in his nostrils. The mill, jetting white steam, grunting, grinding, chugging, giving off a multitude of sounds which mingled into one—which seemed every now and then to be severed by the scream of the saw just as the saw severed the log—lay behind him. It was huge, imposing, with a look of dogged efficiency. He was conscious of a feeling of pride in it.

The gigantic piles reared above him—more than a million feet of timber—rough and rude from the forest—which one day would reappear as homes for the rich and for the poor, in the furniture in those homes, as the cases of pianos and the polished tops of tables; as the cabinets housing that latest of the great marvels, radio. No man might look at any log and foretell its ultimate destination or what it might become. There was wonder in this, something glowing and splendid, something poetic with an epic sweep. Men with cant dogs worked hazardously upon those heights, running about upon curved unstable surfaces, handling adroitly enormous and perverse logs, looping them in chain—great bundles of them—to be snaked across the river to the eater saws. He peered about him to determine who had summoned him, but there was no apparent need; no boss came hastening, no confusion was obvious, no knot of men pointed to the heart of an emergency.

He picked his way across that muddy incline, pausing as a voice, indistinct and invisible, called his name. And suddenly the steeply slanting face of the pile under which he stood was endowed with motion—a rumble, an ominous grunting as log smote log, and leaping, smote log again. A cry of warning sounded in his ears; he leaped. The face of the log pile became an avalanche. Warren stumbled, went to his knees, struggled to his feet again; and then, half crouching as he ran, seemed barely to be touched by a rebounding log—a log which passed on over the spot until it soughed into the stream. And Warren lay, face buried in the mud, with one arm lying at an angle which could not be assumed by an arm whose bones were intact.

The first man to reach his side was James Perrigo! They lifted him and laid him silent upon a spread of coats, while men ran to the mill camp for rude first-aid appliances and to telephone in haste for the doctor. He did not stir or open his eyes, but he breathed, heavily, unpleasantly. Concussion, possibly fracture. . . . The doctor arrived, did what could be done upon the spot, and then a wagon—for there was no ambulance—carried him home as gently as such a wagon could do.

Walter Perrigo reëntered the mill quietly, hung his hat again upon its hook and resumed his position exactly as if it had not been separated from him by Warren Cross less than an hour before. Who knew he had been discharged but himself and Cross? And he doubted greatly if Cross would ever be able to disclose the fact. . . . He was one of the last to be notified of the accident, and listened to the news with becoming solicitude.

CHAPTER XIV

JANET CROSS was alone when they brought her husband home. It is true that Nellie, the hired girl, was somewhere about the house, but Nellie did not seem then to signify as a human being. The old doctor had driven ahead to prepare her, and she had received the news unemotionally—too unemotionally, the doctor thought. He could not see how terrified she was.

"Is he dead?" she asked in a voice that was metallic but did not tremble.

"No. He's hurt bad, but he ain't dead, and won't be if we all keep our heads and don't get flustered."

"I'm—I'm not flustered," she said.

She was not; the impact had been too great for any surface display of nerves. What she felt was cold stark horror—horror that this catastrophe should have befallen here. Colchester multiplied the intensity of it. . . . She recalled that night when, in Warren's absence, Sarah had been seized with acute appendicitis. The terror of that had left its mark upon her mind—in their New York apartment. But in New York help was at hand; the telephone had brought a strange doctor who had ordered Sarah immediately to an impersonal hospital, where a great and efficient—but also impersonal—surgeon had operated. To him Sarah was an incident on his schedule. But, impersonal as it had all been, help was available. Here, in this remote spot, what was one to do? Where was one to turn? There were no hospitals, no ambulances, no nurses, no surgeons—only this old and shabby doctor with the stains of chewing tobacco on his beard. The responsibility was all upon her, and how should she meet it?

"Who you got workin' for you? Nellie, hain't it?" He went to the door and peered into the kitchen. "Go up and get a bed ready for Mr. Cross. He's hurt."

"Bad?" asked Nellie.

"Hold your tongue and do's you're told. . . . And then put on a kittle of hot water."

Janet shrank from his uncouthness, his roughness. On his part he was thankful for Nellie; she was of his own people, and he could depend on her. This girl from New York—what good was she?

They brought Warren in and carried him up to his bedroom; Janet followed blindly.

"You clear out of here," said the doctor, "and when Aunt Hat comes, send her right up."

"I—I want to help."

He scowled. "Help by keepin' from underfoot," he said harshly.

She felt her way downstairs and sat on the bottom step; even through her terror a hatred of Colchester and of its ways made itself felt. She must do something; she could not leave her husband in such hands.

Blindly, without purpose, she got to her feet as the front door was thrust open and a woman's figure entered. It was a strange, grotesque figure of an old woman whom age had not touched with softening finger. Her hair was of an unnatural, shiny, glossy brown. Her lips were thick and her eyes small above the protruding cheek bones, and the skin was patched with yellow. Rather more than the trace of a beard was present. From chin to broad flat feet she was a series of unsightly bulges; almost as broad as she was long, and dressed in black. One was conscious of a corset which seemed to be all wrong and to have been constructed with the express purpose of not fitting the figure upon which it was laced.

"Be you the wife?" this creature demanded.

"I—yes."

"Where is he? Upstairs, eh? Well, how d'ye cal'late I'm goin' to git up—trample over ye?"

She jostled past Janet and waddled up the stairs. What was this new terror, and who was this dreadful apparition? Janet followed, driven by the feeling that she could not leave Warren to be touched by such hands.

But the doctor halted her in the doorway. "I told you to clear out," he said, and turned to the enormity of a woman. "Now, Aunt Hat," he said, "we'll git down to brass tacks."

Janet fumbled her way downstairs again and sank on the lower step. Presently Sarah came, and

Eunice Perrigo; they led Janet to the davenport and sat beside her.

"The doctor's here, of course?" Eunice asked.

"Yes."

"Has Aunt Hat got here yet?"

"Some horrible old woman came—and pushed me out of the way. . . . Oh, I can't bear to leave him with them. What will they do to him?"

"Listen to me," said Eunice firmly. "He's all right with the Old Doc—with the Old Doc and Aunt Hat. They'll lick it, whatever it is. Everything that can be done, they'll do."

"You mean—you'd trust him to—to that frowzy old man and that awful woman?"

"If," said Eunice, "I'm ever terribly ill or dreadfully hurt, I hope it is where they can get to me. There's nobody like them." Her eyes shone. "They —they do miracles!"

Minutes passed—hour-long minutes; and hours— day-long hours. Other people came: Kitty Bridge, who ordered Sarah and Eunice from the house and took charge of domestic affairs. She compelled Janet to take a bit of food—but her principal duty was answering the door. It seemed as if all Colchester came upon that front stoop to make inquiries and to proffer help. Edna Fox came and went into the kitchen; old Mrs. Paget, whom Janet did not even know by sight, brought three freshly baked loaves of bread.

It was not like New York. Even through her dumb misery Janet sensed something different, something kindly, well-meant, sincere. Here was no impersonal ambulance driver or doctor or surgeon or hospital, but solicitude, actual and eager to make itself material. And the doctor! As hour after hour passed and the Old Doc remained in the room with Warren Janet sensed vaguely that her husband was no mere incident on a schedule; not merely raw material for an operation, to be wheeled into the room at exactly ten minutes past ten. Not that—the Old Doc was making a personal fight of it; his interest was in saving this individual, this definite human being; and he fought the fight with all the resources of his skill and experience. It was one of his family who was laid low—a member of his community, and he knew neither time nor weariness in the prosecution of his battle.

Through that first day, and the next and the next, Janet was to learn something of the meaning of friendship, something of the significance of genuine sympathy. Here friends did not call on the telephone perfunctorily to offer sympathy, or send cut flowers from the florist on the corner; they came in person with offers of help—and meant them—and with offerings of a practical kind. Flowers there were, from old-fashioned gardens, but it was the larder which Colchester seemed to consider. Loaves of bread; pots of baked beans, layer cakes, pies, a roast chicken; freshly cut asparagus—so Colchester exhibited its solicitude. Not with engraved cards thrust into boxes ordered by telephone from the hothouse. Colchester did not go through the form of being solicitous; it tried its best actually to do something about it.

Warren Cross remained unconscious; his arm was set and no internal injuries developed; but the concussion—not even the Old Doc could tell whether that condition would subside.

"One thing about these here concussions," said Aunt Hat—"they gen'ally hain't as bad as they look. And if you git well, you do it quick."

"Who is this woman?" Janet had asked. "A trained nurse?"

"She's just Aunt Hat. Trained? Goodness, no! Unless taking care of the sick is training. She dotes on it. If you don't have sickness in the family every so often, or a baby or something, she gets her back up and won't speak to you."

"What do you pay her—I mean, how much?"

"Pay Aunt Hat? Gracious, Mrs. Cross, don't try to do that! She'd blast you! But you can send her a black dress pattern if you want to. Not that she needs it or will ever wear it. I'll bet she's got the stuff to make twenty black dresses in her garret—and the Lord knows what else. Trunkfuls of things! She loves to get little presents, and then sticks them away in trunks and never looks at or uses them. . . .

And don't mind if she calls you Ethel. She calls almost everybody Ethel or Newt—her children's names. She lost them years and years ago."

"Poor old thing!" said Janet.

"I think she's happy. If spending your whole life doing things for somebody else can make you so, then she surely is."

"But how long will she stay?"

"As long as you need her—and she'll leave in a huff. She takes it as a sort of personal slap in the face when her patients get well."

There was one person in Colchester who did not call, and that was Knuckles. But half an hour after Warren's injury he was in the log yard of the mill, prowling about, scrutinizing the particular mountain of logs where the thing had happened and listening to the talk of the men and their arguments as to how the accident had happened. He learned who was on the pile and who was near; he learned that James Perrigo had been on the spot and was the first to reach Warren Cross. . . . As he recrossed the river he encountered James on the bridge, and stopped. James' face was somber; he nodded.

"Can't understand how it happened," said Knuckles.

"He's not dead," said James.

"He could have been. Maybe he will be."

"That," said James, "would be bad."

"I cal'late so—for him."

James lifted his fine eyes and stared for a moment into Knuckles' face, with resentment, not with inquiry, but in a manner peculiar to himself.

"You was there," said Knuckles. "How did it come to happen?"

James shook his head slowly without removing his eyes from Knuckles' face.

"I don't like accidents," Knuckles said, "but they generally come in threes, seems as though. I'd be kind of careful to see the other two don't happen."

"They're bad," said James, and his dark eyes, rather melancholy, looked past Knuckles at the distance. They were inscrutable eyes, but in their depths seemed to reside a great longing. They softened as they moved along the mountain slopes, green and black and yellow with the verdure of countless growing trees. Knuckles wondered what it was they reminded him of; it was not of any man or woman, but of some creature capable alike of gentleness and of ruthlessness.

"You never can tell who'll be the next," Knuckles said. "It might be you or me—or it might be neither of us. It might be somebody you wouldn't think of anythin' happenin' to—except Walter. Accidents don't happen to Walter."

"No," said James.

"It always seems worse when somethin' happens to a woman."

"Yes," said James.

"Like—well, like Eunice, for instance."

There was a brief silence while Knuckles scrutinized James' face, but it did not alter its expression save that he pursed his lips and frowned as if he were concentrating upon some problem.

"I had a dog once that couldn't keep away from porcupines," James said finally. "Always had his nose full of quills, seems as though."

"I've seen such simple-minded dogs."

"Porcupines," said James, "mind their own business. You don't get quills in your nose unless you shove it against them. I've seen them fighting among themselves, and miaowing and all, but they have a family way of doing it. It's just outsiders meddling that get full of slivers."

"That," said Knuckles, "sounds like advice."

It seemed then as if Knuckles passed out of James Perrigo's consciousness; the young man's face lost its expression of gravity; it lightened as from some inward reflection—and so became more inscrutable than ever. The expression of his face seemed to spread throughout his graceful, sinewy body, so that he looked not like a young lumberman clothed roughly for his work, but like something half pagan, half feral, which stood just outside the circle of man's affairs and lived in a dimension not discernible by circumscribed mundane eyes. So he stood for a moment, peering almost joyously across the valley toward its rampart of verdured hills. It was as if they were sending to him some message which he delighted to read. And then, as if Knuckles were not there, he passed on with that sleek, lithe, gliding stride. Knuckles watched him until he disappeared in those foothills of logs, and then, shaking his head, he himself pursued his way toward the village.

CHAPTER XV

EUNICE PERRIGO'S blue runabout stood
waiting outside the bank; Knuckles stood waiting beside the blue runabout. He whiled away the
time by whittling a bit of kiln-dried spruce with a
keen-bladed knife, deftly cutting and shaving until
it took the form of a pair of scissors which opened
and shut. Knuckles was very skillful in such matters. He whistled tunelessly through his teeth, and
one would have said that he had not only the whole
day but all eternity at his disposal. A young man
stopped beside him.

"I hear tell you've swapped yourself into the cider
mill," said the young man.

"Seems as though."

"I got through up to Green's," said the young
man tentatively.

"What you figger your time's wuth?" Knuckles
dropped far into the vernacular. It was the language of trade.

"Green he paid me three dollars a day and found."

"That was before he saw the doctor, wan't it?"
Knuckles asked, with a great lack of interest in his
voice.

"Ol' Man Rea ketched him a speckled trout he

184

claims weighed six pound," said the young man, "up by the Red Bridge."

"That'd make it weigh about three 'n' a half," said Knuckles.

"Them vats needs to be scalded," tendered the young man.

"Not at three dollars and found," said Knuckles.

"Ben Fox's drivin' the oil wagon," said the young man.

"Always did like sittin'-down jobs." He cast his eye into the bank and saw Eunice moving away from the window. "The cider mill's still down yonder," he pointed. "If you can see your way to takin' two-fifty a day and find yourself, the key's on the ledge over the door."

"You've hired a man," said the young fellow; and, before Knuckles could think it over and change his mind, he started at a rapid walk toward his new employment.

Eunice pushed open the door and came daintily down the steps. Knuckles appreciated the slenderness of her ankles, the confident carriage of her shoulders, the pert intelligence of her youthful face. There was something about her other than her beauty which cried out to him—a competence of movement and gesture, a sureness, a lithe grace not unmindful of her brother James. It gave one a feeling that she could do things; that she was able— and Knuckles took off his hat to ability.

She crossed the walk and her chin lifted as she

saw Knuckles. He performed the unusual gallantry of opening the car door for her and received for thanks a little grimace of scorn.

"Good mornin'," he said.

She looked down into his lean brown face—a face by no means handsome, but nevertheless arresting and satisfying to one who may be pleased by clear level eyes, by shrewdness touched with humor, by a lack of expression due to suppression of emotions—which, in itself, gives an intellectual touch. You could not look at Knuckles without feeling that he was, as the local appraisal has it, smart. Nor could you avoid the impact of a certain force, a power of will, and the knowledge that here resides an adroitness to carry out the orders of the will. But Eunice was not looking for these things; her eyes were cold and unfriendly.

"Of all things!" she said in that exasperating tone which young women use to put presumptuous young men in their places.

Knuckles held open the door and she waited for him to remove his hand, but he did not remove it. "Cal'late I'll ride a ways with you if you don't mind," he said.

"You ride with me!" The very unexpectedness of it nonplused her, but she recovered quickly enough to make an acid reply: "That would brighten my day."

"I gather," said Knuckles placidly, "that you wouldn't care for it." His voice became grave and lost all trace of the vernacular. "It is not your company I want, Eunice, and I am not so foolish as to suppose mine could give you pleasure—yet. Suppose we say it is business—important business."

Her attention did not center upon the last sentence, but upon what seemed to her the significant point of the speech. "What do you mean—yet?" she demanded.

"We have lived in the same small place since you were born," he said gravely.

"What of it?"

"Have I ever—personally—done anything you can resent?"

"Just being underfoot is enough for me, thanks. . . . But why the 'yet'?"

"Because I meant 'yet,' " he said, "and you can be thinking it over. Just now there are more pressing things." He smiled saturninely. "Not more important, possibly, but more pressing." With which he stepped into the car and sat down by her side. She glared at him.

"If I were a man ——" she said.

"I am going," he said, "to ride with you and to talk to you. Please drive on. It would have been better to see you privately, but that could not be done in the state of your disposition."

Her cheeks flamed and her eyes flashed; exasperation brought her close to furious tears. "Will—you —get—out?" she said between her teeth.

"How is Mr. Cross?" he asked, and there was something in his voice which arrested—even startled her.

"Still unconscious. What a dreadful accident!"

He turned to face her and spoke very softly; indeed, his voice was little above a whisper. "It was not an accident," he said, "and that is why I must talk with you."

"What do you mean?" she asked; but suddenly she was breathless, frightened by something unknown and ominous.

"Drive," said Knuckles.

The car moved, swished into speed, careened around the corner. They flashed through the village and up the hill toward the lake before either of them spoke again.

"Things," said Knuckles, "are coming to a head."

"What things?"

"Listen," said Knuckles, "and use your head. Put together what you must know and have seen with what I tell you. You," he said, "are nobody's fool." She listened. "We'll start a ways back. Your family sold the mill and timber—why?"

"Against my will," she said.

He nodded. "Did Walter force the sale, or were Walter and James together?"

"I—I don't know. One never knows about James."

"But what do you think?"

"I think it was Walter's idea, and he persuaded James. But it might have been James' idea from the beginning."

"It might. But why did they sell—a profitable business, a family business? What reason?"

"They didn't bother to give me reasons. There was nothing I could do about it."

"But you thought about it."

"I couldn't understand it."

"The agreement was that Walter and James should be retained in their jobs."

"Yes."

"Now—since the mill was sold it has become unprofitable. It has gone downhill—under the same management."

"I don't know."

"Walter—or James and Walter have converted all the Perrigo properties into money."

"I don't know. . . . Not my house and the farms." Her lips set. "They wouldn't dare."

But she was not thinking of the house and farms; with apprehension, she was thinking of that trunkful of money she came upon in Walter's room. . . . Converted all the Perrigo properties into cash, Knuckles had said! Was this a part of the money derived from the sale of the Perrigo properties, or was it some hoard of Walter's derived from some other source? And why was it there at the house and not in a bank? She could think of no honest reason for it. Indeed, she could think of no honest reason for anything Walter did. . . . One may dislike a stranger bitterly, but for real hatred we must look to people of the same blood. In Walter, Eunice could see no good; she despised and suspected him; and latterly, since the discovery of that hoard, she had commenced a little to fear him.

Should she speak of that money? But why? Knuckles was an open enemy of her family. She could not as yet perceive why he had forced this interview upon her, nor what was its meaning. Nevertheless, try as she might to throw it off, she could not dissipate a feeling of security in his presence, a sensation that he was to be trusted; an instinct which told her to place her dependence upon him. But she did not speak. She was shrewd in her way, and the circumstances demanded caution; so she would listen and not speak. When she saw deeper into the matter then she could decide.

"Walter," said Knuckles, "resents your ownership of the house."

"Everybody knows that."

"We must add up so many little facts to get a correct total," Knuckles said.

"But what has all this to do with what you hinted —that it was not an accident to Mr. Cross?"

"I'm working toward that. It was unreasonable to sell the mill—if the intention were to part with it forever. But if—suppose there was someone with a scheming mind, possibly two sharp and scheming minds—who planned to sell a mill, and then, remaining in management, to set it running toward ruin; to engineer happenings so that the property would, in the estimation of its buyers, decline in value!

Suppose Walter—or both of them—sold the mill for a high price, planning to buy it in again as a dead dog."

"You are talking about my brothers," Eunice said stiffly.

"One of them, at least. Have you not said and thought worse of him?"

"What goes on within the family is our business. Anyhow what business is it of yours? You Knuckleses hate us Perrigos."

"That is true of my father. He holds his grudge against you all. I have been raised on it. In this thing I started to get our own back, but ——"

"Yes—but?" she asked.

"But it has gone beyond that, and another element has come in."

"What other element?"

"You," said Knuckles. He did not pause upon this, but went on rapidly. "We'll leave James out, because we haven't solved him, and call it Walter. Walter plans to buy back the mill for a song. He is well on his way to destroying the property in the eyes of purchasers, when something happens to upset his plans."

"What something?"

"Warren Cross comes to town."

She gasped, for she saw the significance of that, coupled with his charge in the beginning that the accident was no accident.

"But ——"

"You can't tell what a man will do—when he is driven into a corner. We don't know how tight a corner Walter may be in. But we do know that when Cross came matters had to move toward a climax. Cross was bound, sooner or later, to discover the truth."

"And did he?"

"He did—the day before he was injured."

Again Eunice gasped. "But—but did Walter know it?"

Knuckles frowned. "There's the weak point. I don't know. I know he found Walter was shipping high-grade lumber on orders which called for low-grade—and pocketing the difference—to a company which is his own in Boston. Did you know that?"

"No."

"Probably formed for the very purpose," said Knuckles. "I know Cross discovered this—a part of it—and was going to discharge Walter and James offhand. I advised against it."

"You! How did you come into it?"

"I think Cross came to a point where he had to confide in somebody."

"So he picked a known enemy of the Perrigos."

"I doubt if that entered his mind."

"I suppose," Eunice said ironically, "it was because you have such a way of inspiring trust."

He turned upon her gravely. "It may be," he said. "I find myself trustworthy. . . . What do you think?"

She hesitated. "I'll make up my mind about that later," she said. "Go on."

"I think—I have studied it out in the light of my observations of Warren Cross—that he did not follow my advice. I introduced an element ———"

"What element?"

"Yourself," said Knuckles quietly.

She frowned. "You always come back to me."

"I'm glad you've noticed it," he said. "I gave the advice I did because of you. He is a conscientious fellow, and may have felt his duty to his employers would not permit other interests to interfere. I believe he confronted Walter with the facts—and discharged him."

"But Walter is still there."

"Exactly," said Knuckles. "And that's the point. I know there was an interview between them. I know that, half an hour later, a telephone call brought Cross out to the log yard. Nobody seems to know who called for him or why. . . . And then it happened. . . . Also we have got to consider this: James was behind the pile from which the log rolled. He was the first to reach Cross afterward."

Eunice felt suddenly very lonely—lonely and frightened by all this. It was dreadful. Her brother —her brothers were actually being charged with an attempt to take a human life. And she was not giving the lie to the man who made the charge. She could not give it the lie. She believed it. It marched with her knowledge of Walter, saving only that she had not assayed him as possessing so much malign resolution. Yet she had seen in him something malign, and it had revolted her. . . . She sat silent and considered.

"James was there?" she asked.

"On the spot."

"Then," she said, "I don't think he had anything to do with it. Whatever Walter might have done— not James."

"Why?"

"If James had been concerned he wouldn't have been there. Oh, I know James better than most. He would have been off in the woods. James is subtle, Ab. He wouldn't be caught like that."

Ab she had called him—unconsciously, it is true. It was a little thing, but he stored it away as a treasure.

"Perhaps," he said. "Perhaps Walter even saw to it James was there."

"Oh!" exclaimed Eunice. That was an evil she could not endure to contemplate.

"I wish," Knuckles said, "I knew that was so— that it was all Walter, and that James and ——"

"James and ——?" she asked.

"—— James and you were to be the victims," he finished.

She was quick to follow to his conclusion. "You mean that Walter wants it all?" she asked.

"What do you think?"

"He wants it," she said, and that was all. She

knew he wanted it; knew he resented her, and that she had been favored by her father.

"Can you add anything to this?" he asked.

She could add so much, but she would not add it yet. After all she was a Perrigo. It was better to be robbed by her brother than to have the name of Perrigo covered with shame. It was better than to ally herself with this enemy of her house. And yet she was allied with him; against her will, it is true, but none the less in alliance. She considered again if she should tell him.

"Not yet," she said.

"Then you know something?"

"I shan't tell you, Ab. . . . Something's got to be done. I don't care how wicked Walter is—or James —they're my brothers. It's got to be stopped, but they must be protected. It mustn't come out."

"If Cross dies ——" said Knuckles.

"He's not going to die. The Old Doc says so, and so does Aunt Hat. They'd know."

"I wonder if Walter has that news?"

"I told him."

"Then," said Knuckles, "we've got to step softly, for things will move. What he means to do must be done before Cross can take a hand again."

"He must be stopped! Oh, this mustn't go any farther! We must stop him!"

Another morsel for Knuckles to treasure! "That," he said, "is why I forced myself on you—to show you things as they are, and to warn you."

"Warn me!"

"To be very careful," he said. He paused. "Eunice, why don't you go away—to Boston or New York—until this thing clears up?"

Her eyes snapped. "I shan't! I'll stay right here!"

"I was afraid you would. . . . You might as well go back now. . . . But watch your step. Confound it, I wish I knew where James stands."

"Either," said Eunice, "he's running the whole thing, or he isn't in it at all."

"I wish you would go away."

"I shan't."

He lifted his shoulders. "I'll get out here," he said. "No need to advertise this ride."

She stopped the car and he alighted, but she did not go on directly. "Ab," she demanded, "why are you mixing in this?"

For the first time he smiled, and she was to remember how his face lightened and became less angular; she was to remember that brief glimpse of the man who hid under that surface of repressions.

"Think it over," he said.

She drove on; but, strangely, her thoughts did not at first busy themselves with the tragic situation in which she found herself. Instead, she was searching diligently for the answer to a personal and private question.

"What did he mean by 'yet'?" she wondered.

CHAPTER XVI

LITTLE knots of men gathered about typewritten notices which appeared in a dozen parts of the mill; these announced to the hands that after the first of the month all wages would be cut 10 per cent. They were signed in typewriting by the Consolidated Lumber Corporation.

Twenty minutes later Walter Perrigo, looking down from his office window, saw the men gather in the yard in animated discussion. This continued for half an hour, when, with one accord, they turned and walked in a body toward town. The strike was on, the mill was still; not a machine moved, not a belt whirred; not a saw sang its song. Walter watched with some satisfaction; then, when the men were well away, he went down into the mill and carefully removed every notice and destroyed it.

Then he sat down and wrote the owners of the mill at length, setting forth the situation, but minimizing it; making it appear that through ill-placed zeal for economy Warren Cross had antagonized the men and brought about labor troubles—something the mill never had experienced under the old régime.

"The situation," he said, "is not serious. I have known all these men for years and feel sure I can straighten matters out in a few days."

He went on to speak of Cross and his condition regretfully, and to say that in the circumstances as they existed he would carry on to the best of his ability; intimating, in short, that it had been a serious order to introduce a stranger, and that if matters were left with him they would presently take on a new and more gracious aspect.

Having mailed this letter he felt well satisfied with himself. He was a stubborn man and knew what he wanted. Perhaps he was more stubborn than intelligent, unless one discounts a certain genius for the devious. When one adds to a natural stubbornness the fact that, once one plunges into a stream, the current will carry him on even if he desires greatly to reach the bank, a better understanding of Walter's conduct thenceforward will be had.

He was one who could plan his own course, but lacked the ability to reason out what course his opponents would follow. He minimized his opponents, which is not wise. He was not exactly frightened by the lengths to which his project had carried him, but he was apprehensive; he was in danger of becoming afraid, of losing his head—and a terrified man is a dangerous man. He will conduct himself with blind savagery to extricate himself from a corner into which his own actions have crowded him; will be guilty of acts of desperation which his original plan had not contemplated. Already he had been guilty of such an action. It had eliminated Warren Cross; but only for a time, if the doctor's reports were to be credited. In the beginning he had undertaken the minor crimes of fraud and trickery; these had crowded him on to something very like murder, and he had gained very little by it—only delay.

But, being a stubborn man, he was determined to persist and to profit by that delay. If he could so contrive that matters went from bad to worse, letting the blame fall upon Warren Cross' shoulders, he might yet arrive at success—if nothing intervened. Cross was still unconscious; he would be a very sick man for some time to come. Before his recovery Walter hoped to carry his plans through to a successful conclusion. But there was more than a mere scheming for money; there was the regaining of what he considered to be his rights, and the satisfying of a hatred, which, in men like Walter Perrigo, may become the ruling passion of life.

He puttered around the office, for among his other vices, he was a putterer; he ate his luncheon, for it was his custom to bring to the mill a box of sandwiches, a piece of pie and a bottle of coffee. Then he puttered through the afternoon and at four o'clock drove into the village. He stopped in the drug store for cigars, where Elmer, the clerk, always eager for conversation, leaned across the show case to make an observation about the weather. Elmer was always confidential, even when he confided in some dripping customer that it was a driving rain.

"Havin' a dry spell," said Elmer in a cautious tone.

"Pretty dry," admitted Walter.

Elmer cleared his throat and looked about as if to make sure none was eavesdropping. "Streams is gettin' low. Fishin's bad."

"So I hear," said Walter, biting off the end of a cigar.

"I didn't know," Elmer hazarded, "that you folks and the Knuckleses had made it up."

"What?" said Walter explosively.

"Everybody's talkin' it," said Elmer. "I see it with my own eyes—Eunice takin' Ab Knuckles for a ride in her car. She must 'a' left him out some'eres, because she come back alone. . . . Heard any news of Mr. Cross today?"

"No," said Walter, but his mind was not at all on Warren Cross.

"The Congregational ladies sent up a basket of flowers after their meetin' today," said Elmer. "I hear Knowles is dickerin' with Smith for the livery— cal'lates to turn it into a garage."

Walter turned away abruptly; he did not frown, because he seldom made use of that expression. His face had been trained to roundness and vagueness, but his eyes glinted. Eunice riding with Knuckles!

"I hear you're shut down," Elmer sent after him in the same secretive tone. "Kind of a strike, eh?"

Walter made no reply, but stepped into his car and drove home more rapidly than was his custom, for he was a conservative driver. . . . Eunice and Knuckles! What was that infernal girl up to now?

He suspected a deliberate intention to aggravate him; it would be like her.

Eunice was not in the house, nor did she arrive until just before supper was called; then she came in with a flurry, flinging her little hat on the seat in the hall and bursting into the dining room.

"I'm famished," she said, dropping into a chair. "Where's James?"

"How do I know where James is? How does anybody know?"

"Oh, you're not your brother's keeper!" said Eunice provocatively.

Walter did not touch the dish before him, but held his round, staring eyes upon his sister as she went about the business of satisfying a healthy appetite. She became conscious of his stare, and it annoyed her.

"Well," she said, looking across the table at him with puckered brows, "what is it now? Why the glare?"

"What's this about Knuckles?" he demanded.

"What's what about Knuckles? And what business is it of yours?" she countered.

"You were riding with him today."

"Was it in the paper?" she asked pertly.

"It wasn't in the paper, and I don't want it to be," Walter said savagely. "What do you think you're doing anyhow? A Perrigo driving around with a Knuckles!"

"It was an even break," she said, "a Knuckles was driving around with a Perrigo."

"Ab Knuckles never does anything without a purpose."

"Few do," said Eunice.

"What did he want?"

"Good company—and he got it."

"One of these days," Walter said ominously, "you'll go too far."

"And what?" asked Eunice.

"And," said Walter, "you'll wish you'd never been born."

She laughed. "I do now—wish I'd never been born into this family. A fine life we live, don't we? Everybody hating everybody else! There was a decent word spoken in this house—once—but I missed it."

"You stay away from Knuckles."

"I'll do exactly as I please about it."

"Chasing after that fellow when you know he's out for our blood!"

"Chasing!" Her eyes blazed.

"Yes, chasing; making a fool of yourself; getting yourself talked about. I won't stand for it!"

Rage was welling up within her; her breath caught in her throat and her heart began to pound. She was afraid she would cry, and to cry would disgrace her. She felt her knees tremble as they always did when her temper was on the point of running away with her discretion.

"Oh!" she breathed.

"Make yourself common! You little fool, he was trying to pump you! What did you say to him? What did you talk about?"

She gripped her hands together and stared down at her plate, fighting for self-control. What did they talk about! It all flashed through her mind now; they had talked about him—Walter. And how she despised him! How she hated him!

"By dad!"—Walter was always conservative in his oaths—"by dad, I'll show you I'm running this family! You might have been father's favorite, but you're not mine. Maybe you could sneak around him to get the best of it, but I'm boss of this place and of you for a year yet. . . . If I ever hear of your chasing after that man Knuckles again—like a waitress from the hotel ——"

"You—you ——"

"Disgracing this family!"

Suddenly she was cold; her knees trembled still, but her eyes were not threatened by tears. How she hated him! Reason was not in her, nothing but a seething, welling rage, a desire to hurt, to tear him to shreds with words, to punish him with her tongue. She leaped to her feet and flung her napkin across the table.

"Disgrace the family—me! . . . You cheat! You coward! You—you crook!"

"What?" Walter, too, was on his feet now, white

to the lips. "That's Knuckles. What was he saying to you? What dirty lies?"

She laughed again, unpleasantly. She was unconscious of herself save only as a vague third person beside whom she stood to watch and listen. She was even a little appalled at what that third person said and did—a little frightened. But she was helpless to interfere.

"You talk about my disgracing the family! At any rate I'm honest. I've never disgraced the family by stealing—by killing somebody."

Walter breathed through his teeth and slowly commenced to move about the table toward her; she backed away, keeping that barrier between them.

"Disgrace! Prison will be disgrace enough— when you're caught. And you will be caught. Oh, I hope you will! Cheating and lying and plotting! Who did you hire to roll that log down on Warren Cross? You never would dare do it yourself!"

She wanted to stop, wanted to hold back the words, but they overpowered her, compelled her to speak them. It was as if they lived and were possessed of a will superior to hers.

"Robbing the men you work for! Planning to rob me—and James. Oh, I know! I know it all, every bit of it! And you dare talk about disgrace to me! You murderer!"

Walter was very still, but his eyes never left her face. His shoulders were thrown forward and hunched together in a sort of animal crouch; his face was a pasty white and his pale eyes glowed with unsightly, subterranean fires. Slowly, slowly, he moved along the table's edge; slowly, slowly, she kept pace with him.

"You want it all!" she cried. "You want mine and you want James'! Are you planning to kill us too? Have you hired somebody to do that for you? Well, I'm not afraid. And now that I know, I'll beat you. Cheat me!" Her laugh arose shrilly. "I'll show you! I'll show you!"

She could hear his teeth grind together; there was something starkly bestial in his expression now, in the glare of his eyes, in the movement of his body. But still she could not stop.

"Oh, I know it all—everything! And you threaten me! What you'll do to me! I can do a little threatening myself!" She fought to keep the next words back, put her teeth together, but they were inexorable in their demand to be spoken. "What about that trunk?" she cried hoarsely. "Suppose I told about that—that trunkful of stolen money! Thousands and thousands of dollars of it! What if I told about that?"

Walter stood still for an instant, as still as if frozen, and then he stretched an arm out on either side and commenced to draw the table away from her, to swing it aside. Eunice clung to it, terrified now, appalled by what her temper had done. With a sudden wrench he flung the table sidewise, and then he advanced upon her. She gave back, step by step, as he came. In the room now was only a dreadful, menacing silence—the soft rubbing of feet over the carpet, the sibilant indrawing of breath. She was at the wall, felt it touch her shoulders, and she could have screamed. She could give back no more, and he continued to advance. His fingers almost touched her, and she cried out once, shrilly.

Then the door opened, and James stood framed there, eyeing them with inscrutable eyes.

"James!" she cried. "James!" and tottered toward him, tottered and swayed as a pleasant darkness ingulfed her. She did not know that James caught her and held her, and turning those unfathomable eyes of his upon his brother, lifted his shoulders slightly.

"Well," he said, "that's that."

CHAPTER XVII

WALTER PERRIGO was again on an even keel. Events had crowded him so that he had been in danger of losing that calm which is so essential to the successful conduct of an involved plan. One must keep an unflurried mind and a resolution backed by cold judgment, and he had been gravely in danger of losing both. In short, Walter had discovered what it was to be frightened; for a short time it had seemed to him that his actions had collected behind him in a sturdy mass and, with their shoulders against his back, were jostling him to the brink of a precipice. But the sun was shining again.

True, there were still clouds in the west, ominous clouds, but he fancied he had the magic with which to dispel them. Give him time now—a few days, a week, two weeks at most—and he believed he could bring it off with glowing success; even to a success he had not contemplated.

This optimism was due to two causes—he had added a new factor to his plan, and there had arrived an official of the Consolidated Lumber Corporation to look into conditions. The plan carried Walter a step farther than he had contemplated going, and was not a nice plan according to the standards of more ethical gentlemen. But it seemed necessary,

which was sufficient for Walter. It involved a maxi-
mum of treachery, and against one of his own blood;
but if well contrived and efficiently carried through,
it would free him of all suspicion and leave his hands
unstained. James was to be the object of these
attentions.

As to the arrival of Mr. Woodson of the Consolidated Walter had come through with colors nailed
to the masthead. He had rather anticipated some
such visit and was ready. He met Mr. Woodson at
the station and escorted him to the mill, where, for a
long day, they conferred. In this conference Walter
had but one object, and that was to avert the sending
of a substitute for Warren Cross—and he succeeded.
Indeed, he did rather better than that.

"Mr. Woodson," he said, "I'm relieved that you've
come to see exactly how things stand."

"I'm worried about Cross," Woodson said. "That
was a terrible thing, and I feel responsible in a way,
for I recommended that he be sent here. You feel
sure he is out of danger?"

"The Old Doc says so," Walter said. "And it was
a great relief to me. A fine man, Cross. It was a
difficult position for him, but I must say for him that
no man could have handled it more fairly. Naturally
I knew there was dissatisfaction with my management—due, as I shall show you, to events which I
should have controlled very soon—but there was
never friction between Cross and myself. A fine
young man and an able young man."

"He's all of that."

"The big mistake," Walter said, "was in changing the ownership of the mill. We should never have sold, and you should never have bought."

"Perhaps."

"Fact, and I've regretted it. I was more or less forced into it by my family. You see we're queer folks up here; clannish and a little ingrowing. This mill was a sort of town affair. Perrigos ran it and half the town was supported by it. We knew every man, and most of them had worked for us since the day they commenced working. It was second nature with them to work for the Perrigos."

"I suppose there's something in that."

"A great deal. . . . The town resented our selling to you. People felt we had no right to sell. We're a queer lot," he repeated. "I suppose they thought they had some sort of vested right." He laughed. "My brother and I were in bad with everybody."

"I see."

"Well, that's where production dropped. They would work their heads off for the old mill—it was second nature to them. But you folks brought in something of the notion of absentee landlordism. That's the idea. Their backs were up."

"I see," repeated Mr. Woodson.

"It hit every place. People we bought supplies from wouldn't make the same deals they made with us. They as good as said strangers owned the mill, so let's sting them. You know how it is."

"I do," Mr. Woodson said grimly.

"And there was even a little active deviltry—especially in the woods. It was a bad mess."

"It was," Mr. Woodson agreed.

"It seemed to me," Walter said, "the only course was to take it easy. When they saw they were being treated just as we used to treat them, and they were still, in effect, dealing with us Perrigos, I figured they would slip back into the old habits and sort of forget about you folks. It was commencing to work out. I feel we would have been back where we were in another six months. I know it."

"You're making a case," said Mr. Woodson.

"I should have come down to see you," Walter said regretfully, "but my hands were pretty full right here. Naturally you didn't understand, not being on the ground—and then Cross came. That tipped the bucket over again. It waved the fact of absentee ownership—corporation ownership—in their faces again. Now it's all to do over again."

"Cross was told to be diplomatic."

"And he was. People took to him, but as an individual. They resented him as a representative of a foreign corporation. No man could have done more than he, nor done it better. But they got it into their heads he was sent to kick us Perrigos out, and they didn't like that. The idea of having to deal with strangers sort of disturbed them. But I think this unfortunate accident has done away with a great deal of that."

"You mean?"

"Why, as I say, folks liked him. And when this happened, with him up here away from old friends and all, the town was mighty sorry for his little wife. Sympathy does a lot to do away with resentment."

"Um—and this strike?"

"Well, that was the only act of Cross' I could criticize. It wasn't just the time to cut wages, even if that seemed a necessary course. When he had those notices of a 10 per cent cut posted, they just walked out."

"I'm surprised. It doesn't sound like Cross to use that sort of judgment."

"Probably," said Walter, "he was worried, and wanted to get results on the jump. After all he's a young man. And when he was hurt and the order was out, I was powerless. I think I could get the men back in a week or so if I had authority to put wages back."

"By all means," said Mr. Woodson.

"Probably it will be five or six weeks—maybe more —before he will be able to be around again."

"Undoubtedly." Woodson considered. "I thought of sending another man up temporarily; but, in the circumstances, I guess you'd better carry on. Then we'll see."

"The mistake," Walter repeated, "was in selling to you. I wish we hadn't done it."

"As things have turned out," Woodson said, "I'm not sure I don't agree."

"Um—I don't suppose you folks would consider a resale."

"Well, it's a new thought."

"My family wouldn't come in. As I say, they forced my hand. But I'm sure I could finance the thing. There's money around this town. I'd have to show them something of a bargain though. Hard-headed citizens. . . . This mill ought to be run locally."

"All mills should be," said Mr. Woodson, "but it isn't always practical."

"And," said Walter, "there's such a thing as mini-mizing a possible loss."

"We might clean the whole place out and import labor."

"I wouldn't do that," cautioned Walter. "Well, that was just a thought. Consider it, Mr. Woodson, and let me know. Meantime I'll stir around and see about some financing."

"I'll take it up with the board," Mr. Woodson said.

Toward the end of the day he called upon Janet Cross to inquire after her husband and to express his sympathy. He was a brusque man, and business-like. She could not escape the thought that his call did not flow from a deep and sincere sympathy, but was rather a matter of form. His solicitude and proffer of any assistance he could give were of a hollow sound, and she was not sorry when he left to catch his train.

Nor, when he was gone, could she prevent herself from contrasting his call with the calls of the Bridges and the Foxes and the Knowleses and the Hewitts— with the calls of utter strangers with baskets on their arms and real friendship in their eyes. She could not but remember that Aunt Hat had scarcely left the house an instant, and that she dared offer no payment to the queer old woman except a black dress pattern. If it had happened in New York! Her mind played with the idea. How many of her friends would have given up their bridge, their theater, their pleasant occupations to come and virtually take off her hands all the care of her household, as Kitty Bridge and Edna Fox had done? And as for Nellie —she could well imagine how a servant in New York would very likely have left at the first intimation of trouble and of extra work. But it might have been one of Nellie's own family.

She remembered her terrible loneliness at the realization that her husband was frightfully injured in this out-of-the-way place; how she had longed for doctors at the end of the telephone and competent ambulance surgeons and splendid hospitals.

Sarah came in. "I wonder where Eunice is. I haven't seen hide or hair of her today," she said.

"You've seen enough of her every other day," Janet said with a hint of a smile.

"She's a dear," said Sarah. "But one feels sorry

for her. I guess she has a pretty dreadful time at home."

"If I'm any judge," Janet said, "she sends as good as she gets. . . . And you don't seem to find her family so objectionable."

"Oh, James!" Sarah said airily. "He's like keeping a pet. But not a lap dog, my dear, not a lap dog. He's got me winging. I never saw one just like him."

"Then look out," Janet said. "It's bad when they puzzle you. Beware of a handsome and inscrutable young man—and propinquity."

"Don't you worry," Sarah said. "I can roll my own little hoop. And don't you ever think, my dear, that I'm going to cook any man's biscuits so far from Forty-second and Broadway. My idea of the ultimate thing in country is an estate on Long Island."

"Maybe some good'll come out of this awful mess," Janet said. "It may mean our pulling out of here."

"It's not so bad," Sarah said unexpectedly. "I've had a pretty ripping time."

"Novelty, child, novelty. It'll wear off. You can't spend your life slumming up a trout stream with James Perrigo."

"You never were up a trout stream with him," Sarah said cryptically. "It's got its points."

"Does he ever talk? If he does I've missed it."

"When he does," said Sarah, "it isn't chatter. And I'll say this without fear of successful contradiction—he looks the part."

"What part, honey?"

"Don't be sill. He looks the way a man that fools around the woods all the time ought to look."

"In the movies," Janet jeered.

"Movies nothing! James is all on the up-and-up."

"I wonder he understands you when you talk. What's that—night-club English?"

Sarah disregarded that gibe. "Ren warned me off him the night of the fry. I wonder what he was getting at. It wasn't just a dirty dig—he had something on the little old mind."

"Just couldn't see you living up a tree and spending your days hanging from a limb."

"I can imagine worse things," Sarah said, and there was a trifling edge on her voice. "I'm not a fluff, you know."

"I don't know what you are," Janet said good-humoredly, "but I know what you look."

"Go on, darling, be frank."

"You look," said Janet, "like a 1927 model with all the accessories. And you've got to run on asphalt pavements."

"That," said Sarah, "is my virtuous intention—and that sounds like James. That's one thing I like about him—you can always tell when he's in the offing, so you can duck if you want to. I wonder if he whistles in his sleep."

"I'd find out," Janet said significantly. "Personally I'd prefer a snore."

"Be yourself," Sarah said shortly, and walked

toward the front door, arriving there just as James Perrigo came abreast of the house.

"I heard the dicky bird singing," she said jauntily.

He paused and regarded her gravely. "And you came out," he said disconcertingly.

"Well, I like that! Just come around some time and whistle for me and see what happens!"

"Was I whistling?" he asked.

She ignored the question. "Where's Eunice?" she asked.

He paused before answering and seemed to consider. "At home," he said.

"I haven't seen her today."

"She was sick this morning," James said gravely.

"Oh, I wish I'd known. I'd have gone up hours ago."

"When Eunice is sick—stay away," James said sententiously.

"Why?"

"She wouldn't let you in; she won't let anybody in."

"Anyhow I'll give it a try tomorrow."

"I wouldn't," said James.

She laughed. "You are funny," she said.

He moved a step closer. "Are you coming out?"

"Are you coming in?"

"It's better out there." He pointed. "I don't like to talk to you in a house. . . . Were you expecting me?" He could be very disconcerting.

"This is the first time today I've remembered there was such a person," she said.

His eyes smiled—an appealing, a touching, a gentle smile—and he nodded his head. "I don't wonder," he said. "But I remember you." He paused and regarded her until she blushed. "You've never been out there," he said suddenly, waving his hand at the distant forest. "You've never seen it. I want to spend a whole day with you there. It makes a difference. I could talk to you out there."

"You do quite well here," she said uncomfortably.

"I could do better. I could tell you things." He smiled. "I've never wanted to tell anybody things before." He smiled again and drew a step closer. "I'd like to watch you—to sit and watch you all day —out there. I like to look at you."

"Thank you, sir, she said," Sarah told him ironically. "And me with the make-up going stale."

"Will you come some day?—tomorrow?"

"Not tomorrow. I must go and hold Eunice's fevered hand."

"You won't see her," he said. "I tell you, you won't be let in."

"Then I'll crash the gate," she said.

"Not that gate," he answered, and she felt that there was some weighty significance to his words. It puzzled and irritated her.

"Come for a walk?" he asked earnestly.

She lifted her shoulders. "And you can teach me to know the wild flowers," she said.

"I think," he said gravely, "we can teach each other to know a great many things."

She made a little face. Here was one young man her efficient training had not equipped her to handle. He did not recognize a fence when he came to one. It was not without a tingle of apprehension that she looked down at him. But it is worth recording that she descended the steps and walked docilely off among the trees with James at her side.

CHAPTER XVIII

KNUCKLES trudged down the River Road at the edge of the village until he reached a big yellow house, one of a set of buildings, including barn and woodshed, which bore across its front a sign which announced that lodging, victualing and baiting could be obtained here. He turned in and went to the back yard, where a fat man with a blond mustache and red face was chopping firewood. This individual dropped his ax with evident pleasure; it was plain to be seen that he welcomed Knuckles' arrival—not because he delighted in Knuckles' society, but because it gave him a logical excuse to lay down the ax. He mopped his shock of red hair and expelled a great breath between his thick lips.

"How be ye?" he asked graciously.

"Middlin'," said Knuckles, and regarded the woodpile with interest. "Um—made arrangements to get in your winter wood yet?"

"Hain't found jest the right day to git at it yit," said the proprietor of the lodging house. "What with one thing and another, I don't git a minute, seems as though."

"How much you cal'late on usin'?"

"Twenty-five-thutty cord."

"I swapped for Newman's saw the other day," Knuckles said.

"Goin' into the wood business?"

"Cal'late to. . . . Keep the house full, Jed?"

"No complaints; they come and go. Hain't no money in it, not at the prices I kin git. What I make on the lodgin' I lose on the victualin'."

"Who you got?"

Jed named half a dozen employees of the mill who were his guests.

"Thought Latzo lived here."

"He got through to the mill."

"Got through, eh?"

"Yestiddy, kind of sudden-like. James Perrigo, he stopped here last evenin', and near's I kin gather, him and Latzo had words. I couldn't ketch what about. But right after he come in and packed his turkey and paid up and started off up the road."

"James Perrigo?" asked Knuckles.

"James," said Jed.

"Um—I can make you a price on that wood."

"I'd as soon buy off of you as anybody."

They haggled over price, agreed, and presently Knuckles walked back again toward the village, considering information other than he had expected to glean. Latzo was gone. That was not altogether unexpected, for the situation seemed to call for the man's removal to other and unspecified regions. But James Perrigo! Latzo left hurriedly after a discussion with James! Knuckles would not have been surprised to happen upon a secret interview between Latzo and James, and certainly not between the top piler and Walter. But that James should have come openly to the lodging house and have talked openly with the man, and so obviously have ordered him to absent himself from the vicinage—that gave Knuckles toothsome food for consideration.

For Mr. Latzo was the laborer who had been handling logs on the top of the pile under which Warren Cross had suffered injury!

He wedded these facts with the significant fact that James had been adjacent to the pile, so adjacent that he had been first to reach Warren Cross as he lay unconscious. They added up to a baffling total. It was too patent. Either Knuckles had overestimated James Perrigo—or something else. An astute man who plans a catastrophe to one of his fellow men does not make himself prominent at the scene of action; nor does he, openly and in broad daylight, approach his agent of destruction to tell him the air of the locality has become unhealthful—not if he be astute.

It gave a choice of explanations; either James was not at all astute, but a very fatuous miscreant, or he was not a miscreant at all and the victim of malign circumstantial evidence. Or—and upon this possibility Knuckles paused and pondered—the whole scheme was more adroit than even he had imagined, and these appearances of James were vouchsafed for a definite purpose. Somehow he inclined to this point

of view, though there was nothing upon which to
support it; nothing except his firm belief that James
was far from being fatuous and very close to being
astute. But where did this leave Walter?

Perhaps Walter was being driven past his speed.
Knuckles could see Walter as the hero of any chi-
canery, but could not see him in the perilous rôle of
a suborner of violence—unless he were crowded by
circumstances into the condition of a cornered rat.
Then, he fancied, Walter would squeal shrilly and
fight foully. James, in Knuckles' mind, was taking
shape as the leader of the enterprise; Walter was
demoted to the position of a follower who was being
led into water too deep and cold and swift for his
more conservative taste.

He reached the bank corner just as Sarah Cross,
in Warren's car, came down the hill. He did not
see her until she drew up beside the walk and spoke:
"Mr. Knuckles."

"Yes'm," Knuckles said, but without lifting his
hat.

"Warren is conscious."

"Come to, eh?"

"Early this morning. He keeps asking for you.
Of course nobody is allowed to see him, but he seems
so upset and so terribly anxious to see you that both
the doctor and Aunt Hat thought it would be good
for him if you would spare him a few moments."

"To be sure," Knuckles said. "Um—conscious,
eh? Other folks know it?"

"Mrs. Bridge was there."

"There yet?"

"Yes."

"Goin' home now?"

"Yes."

He opened the door and stepped in, asking no further questions. Sarah did not speak for a moment; she was frowning and distrait. "This is a funny town," she said presently.

"I've heard it said," agreed Knuckles.

"I just came from Perrigos'."

Knuckles pricked up his ears. "Go there often, don't you?"

"Quite. But I'm not so sure I'll go again."

"Have words with Eunice?"

"No."

"I'd kind of overlook 'em if I did," said Knuckles.

"I didn't see her," said Sarah.

"Wan't at home?"

"She's sick," said Sarah. "James told me yesterday, and I told him I would go right up."

"How'd that strike James?"

"Queerly."

Knuckles turned now and eyed her keenly. "Queerly—how?"

"He said when Eunice was under the weather she didn't like anyone around—didn't want anybody in the room—probably wouldn't let me in. I told him nonsense!"

"And went?"

"Just now. That scrawny housekeeper of theirs answered the door; opened it about an inch and put her long nose through the crack and said Eunice was in bed and nobody could come in. I told her to take up my name, and she said names didn't make any difference, that nobody could come in. And that's a fine way to treat a friend. So I came away, and it'll be a balmy summer evening before I go back again."

"I don't know's I'd hold it against Eunice," Knuckles said, and relapsed into such concentration that, although Sarah spoke to him three times in an effort to draw his attention, he did not hear her at all. They arrived at the house and alighted. Janet met them at the door.

"I'm so glad you've come," she cried. "Ren is tossing about and working himself into a fever. The doctor thought it would be safer to let him see you. It's an obsession. I—I —— Oh, it was such a relief to have him open his eyes and recognize me." She stood with tears running down her tired cheeks. "It—you don't think it's—delirium or something, do you?"

"Never heard anybody called delirious for wantin' to see me," Knuckles said dryly.

Janet conducted him up the stairs and into Warren's bedroom. The injured man lay upon his back, his eyes upon the door hungrily. When Knuckles entered he sighed and closed his lids for an instant and his lips moved spasmodically.

"Now don't git into a stew," said Aunt Hat peremptorily. "He's here." She turned accusingly to Knuckles. "He's been bawlin' for you like a calf separated from its mother."

"He's got suthin' on his mind that it's better he got off," said the Old Doc.

"Seems as though," said Knuckles. "Cal'late it's private." He looked at the door. "Doc, who you told he was conscious?"

"Nobody."

"Kitty Bridge downstairs?"

"Yes."

"Tell her not to tell anybody." He motioned toward the door.

"Use discretion," admonished the Old Doc. "I'll come back when you been here long enough."

Knuckles went over and sat on the bed; Warren looked up into his face with burning eyes. "What's —happened?"

"Nothin'."

"Who's—in—charge?"

"Walter."

Warren struggled as though to arise, but groaned and lay still with his eyes closed. "I—fired—him."

"Guessed it," said Knuckles.

"You—take—job." Warren's voice was weak; it was a struggle to force the words. "Throw—him —out."

Knuckles sat with bent brows, unconscious of the burning, feverish, pleading look which Warren directed upward to his face. He was considering, fitting this into place in the jig-saw puzzle, estimating its uses and its disadvantages.

"Guess I better," he said finally.

"You—write"—Warren paused a long time between scarcely audible words—"authority—I'll—sign."

Knuckles understood, and could admire the fortitude and resolution of this young man, who, just emerged from the shadows, could still compel his dazed and battered brain to function; who had place in his thoughts for no worry, no fear, nothing but to keep faith with those whose servant he was; who forgot self but remembered loyalty and duty. Knuckles did not speak of it then, nor, being what he was and of the blood he was, would he refer to it in the future; but he gave ungrudging admiration, storing away in the recesses of his mind the certainty that here lay a man worthy to come and to go with.

He scribbled rapidly with fountain pen in notebook and stepped to the door.

"We're through," he said. "Come in. Need witnesses. You, Doc, hold his hand while he makes his mark as best he can. It says: 'This authorizes Abner Knuckles to assume full authority over the mill and property of the Consolidated Lumber Corporation in and about Colchester; to hire and to discharge, buy and sell.' That what you want, Cross?"

"Yes."

They contrived a scrawling, all but illegible signature, but with witnesses. Knuckles touched Warren's uninjured hand. "Be content," he said.

Warren closed his eyes and sighed—sighed like a child who long has cried for something denied him when the boon at last is granted. Knuckles walked to the door.

"This," he said, "comes under the head of professional secrets."

On the front stoop Sarah waited for him. "I'll drive you back," she said.

"I'll contrive to walk," he answered abstractedly. He turned not toward the mill with his newly undertaken position and his written authority, but toward the village; and he made his way slowly. It was one thing to possess authority; it was another thing to choose the hour and the moment for exercising it. He deemed the hands of the clock were in the wrong position just now—and so Walter remained intrenched and confident and optimistic for yet a few hours. For Knuckles was not troubled about Walter, but about James.

As for Sarah, she was presently glad that Knuckles had refused her offer of a ride, for James appeared from nowhere and turned in at the gate. She received him with that austerity which an injured young woman knows so well how to assume, and he eyed her curiously, but not apprehensively.

"I'll come for you early tomorrow," he said.

"I'm not sure I want to go," she said coldly.

"I want you should," he said. That was all.

There was no pleading, no argument, merely a flat statement of his wishes; but even as she resented it, she knew she would comply.

"They wouldn't let me in," she said angrily.

"No," said James.

"What kind of a way is that to act?"

He did not answer for a moment, but those dark, fine, inscrutable, daring, appealing eyes of his seemed to search her face for some necessary information.

"A little brook, runnin' through the woods and fallin' over rocks," he said. "There's pools—and you can sit and listen to it. Did you ever sit and listen to a brook? Folks ought to listen to brooks more. You can think. And it's pretty. Music is just a pretty noise, but the brook plays the prettiest of all."

His voice stilled her resentment, quieted her, soothed her until her hard young eyes became gentle, wistful.

"I don't see how you could live in a city," he said.

"I managed all right," she said with a little nervous laugh.

"You're not for cities. Just your clothes—not you. You lived there because you didn't know. But I'm going to show you. There's nothing in a city for you."

"Is that so?" She sought to regain her poise and to assert herself. "I think I could do with a few good theaters, and music, and places to dance, and people who knew what fork, and shops and taxis and men who wear their coats and aren't all called Jim or Bill or Pazzy."

"You won't miss them," he said. "Colchester, without the woods and the mountains, would be better than that; but there are always the woods and the mountains."

"You should have pointed ears and hoofs," she jeered.

"New York," he said, "would pare away the hoofs of Pan and nail on shoes—and set him to drawing away ashes in a cart."

"At least he would be useful."

"Being useful," said James, "is spoiling the world. I must be useful, you must be useful, this must be useful, that must be useful. And then we die, and this and that is used up and destroyed—and we have wasted our time."

"You can talk!" Sarah said pertly.

James smiled. "I can talk, I can look, I can listen, I can feel—and that is to live. But it's not useful. Useful things last a day—and then the scrap heap. It is only the useless that lives forever; a song, or a couple of dozen words brought together into a poem."

"I guess I'll go," Sarah said abruptly.

"Of course," he said, as if no other possibility ever had occurred to him. And this time, strangely enough, she did not resent it.

CHAPTER XIX

KNUCKLES pushed back his chair and stood looking across the red-and-white checked tablecloth at his father.

"Goin' out?" asked Mr. Knuckles, without moving his lips. It was so he always spoke and, as each year passed over his head, the characteristic was growing upon his son.

"Walk around a spell," said Knuckles.

"You was drivin' with that girl," said the old man.

"It's gen'ally known," Knuckles said dryly.

"She'll bamboozle ye into lettin' 'em off easy."

"Maybe, but I don't think it."

"Be you serious with her, Ab?" There was something appealing in the old man's voice.

"Yes," Knuckles said directly.

"Have ye asked her?"

"No."

"Us Knuckleses is set in our ways." The father conformed his lips and stared up at his son with unbending sternness.

"So it's said."

"I couldn't abide it. . . . A Knuckles and a Perrigo!"

"We're comin' close to the end," Knuckles said, but with no air of changing the subject. "They're bein' crowded into a corner. . . . Cross is conscious."

"Um——"

"I'm goin' to walk around," Knuckles said, and putting on his hat, went out of the door.

He walked to the northward until he came to a lane which ran in lonely fashion up the hill between stone walls—stones gathered by infinite toil from the fields on either hand. Up this lane he turned, sauntering, until presently he sat down beyond a clump of sumac bushes and lighted his pipe. The shadows lengthened and the sun submerged itself in the clouds to the westward, but Knuckles continued to smoke until the dusk was deepening to darkness. Then he got to his feet again, and walking somewhat more swiftly, ascended the hill, leaped the wall and, keeping to the shelter of witch hopple and sumac which grew hedgelike between the fields, he continued until he arrived at a point at the right of the Perrigo house—a point from which he could see both front and rear entrances, and from which he could be certain not to miss anyone who came or went.

He did not smoke now, but lost himself in the small growth and waited. Patience was a quality which served him well, for an hour passed, two hours; there was no sign of life outside the house, but a light glowed from James' window and from that part of the building where the housekeeper slept. Knuckles could see Eunice's window, but there was no light there—a fact which gave him food for reflection.

There should have been a light. If Eunice were not sick, but merely ailing, she would require a light by which to read; if she were very ill, those who cared for her would require a light. He guessed that she was not occupying her own room, and wondered why.

But now his ear, which served even better than his eyes, demanded all his attention. He listened. Undoubtedly someone was moving behind him; someone who breathed heavily and who stumbled over hillside stones which the darkness concealed. Knuckles pressed more deeply into the shelter of the bushes—and the man passed him, not a dozen feet away. Knuckles, even in that scant moonlight, recognized that hat, those great swinging shoulders and the bulky movement of the thighs. It was the man Latzo.

Latzo paused briefly, scrutinizing the house; and then, with cautious movements made his way across the yard to a point directly under Walter's window, against which he threw a handful of gravel. Walter's head appeared.

"Is it you?" Walter asked in a whisper that, nevertheless, carried to Knuckles.

"Who'd you s'pose?" Latzo demanded truculently.

"Go to the back door. I'll let you in."

There was silence for a space, then the rear door opened and shut and Latzo was inside. Here was highly seasoned food for thought. Knuckles had not taken the trouble to prowl up the hill and to lurk in the bushes with any hope of overseeing such an occurrence as this. His interest had been in Eunice Perrigo and her illness, and he had come to see if he could not get some news as to her health. It is often, however, that the by-products save the firm from bankruptcy. So far he had increased his knowledge of Eunice's condition by very little; he had deduced that she was not occupying her own room, which was something, but certainly not enough upon which to base a biography. But this appearance of the missing Mr. Latzo and his fraternizing with Walter were significant. It was significant of something, but just what Knuckles was hardly prepared to say. He awaited further enlightenment.

It came presently. Walter emerged from the door and held it open; then appeared something resembling a huge turtle walking on its hind legs, and Knuckles deduced that Latzo was impersonating the turtle. He strained his eyes to see what was impersonating the shell, and in the increasing moonlight made it out to be a small flat trunk. He did not recognize the trunk; but Eunice would have done so at once, for it was the trunk which had been on her mind constantly since the night of the flat-rock fry. Knuckles was far from perceiving the significance of the box, but did not lack the astuteness to reach the conclusion that it was highly significant.

"It ain't heavy," Latzo said.

"Where's the wagon?"

"Down a piece."

"Be sure you keep it in a dry place," Walter cautioned. "It's full of papers."

Full of papers! Knuckles listened to that; and knowing Walter as he did, made sure in his mind that, whatever the trunk contained, it was not documents; also Mr. Latzo was not meant to know the character of his burden.

"And keep out of sight," said Walter.

"I'll stay right there," said Latzo.

"Till I come," Walter said.

"He's always snoopin' around some'eres," said Latzo.

Knuckles wondered if himself was meant by this accented "he"; that seemed logical. He was, indeed, always snooping around; at the moment he was indulging in the avocation.

"I don't want anybody to see that trunk—anybody," said Walter.

"If he comes nosin' around, it'll be alone," Latzo said significantly.

When Walter spoke again Knuckles was compelled to revise some of his estimates of that gentleman; it was not the voice of the Walter he knew, but of a vastly more determined Walter, a more malignant Walter, a greatly more venturing Walter. Knuckles rubbed his chin and had difficulty restraining a little whistle of astonishment.

"I wouldn't miss him," said Walter. That was all, but it was eloquent. It was malign, callous, coldly calculating.

"Somebody would," said Latzo.

"I got that end of it in hand," said Walter. "It fits in. If he turned up missing folks would believe he absconded. I can prove it."

Absconded! If someone was reported missing his absence would be accounted for as a criminal flight! It might be Knuckles they were discussing, but this made it seem less probable. Knuckles cudgeled his mind to see how Walter could make him appear an absconder, but the problem was beyond him. But if not himself, then who?

A fixed idea, a preconception arrived at by logic, is sometimes a dangerous thing. It obscures the view like some thick fog and envelops the facts in a grayness which hides their features. Knuckles was the victim of such a preconception, and instead of enlightenment from this conversation, he was only plunged more inextricably in perplexity. So far as he could see Walter had reason to be afraid of only two persons—himself and Warren Cross. Cross was disposed of for the time being, so that only Knuckles remained. But the absconding! With what could he possibly abscond?

"Maybe I can arrange it so he does come," Walter said. "Now don't you be seen going back. You're out of this part of the country. And lay low."

"Lower'n a snake's stummick," said Latzo reassuringly.

"Better be on your way. And don't get caught with your eyes shut."

"Not me."

"And don't let anybody see that trunk—especially him."

"Huh!" grunted Latzo.

He swung his burden again to his enormous shoulders and stepped easily across the grass plot, a huge man, curiously magnified and distorted by the moonlight, advancing with the appearance of some malignant gnome. Walter stood briefly looking after him and then went in, closing the door softly after himself.

Knuckles crouched low and held his breath while Latzo passed within a dozen feet of him; then he turned to watch the man's progress across that bowlder-strewn pasture. He was of two minds whether to follow him or not, because that trunk had seized upon all his curiosity. But he decided against it. Latzo would not go far, and Walter was always there. When the time came, by keeping his eye on Walter he could always come to Latzo and the trunk. And the bare knowledge of this incident would be very helpful. It would enable him to pretend to knowledge which he did not possess. So he crouched silently, while Latzo traversed the field, climbed a distant wall and was lost to sight among the sumacs bordering the road.

CHAPTER XX

SARAH CROSS was not accustomed to being up at the hour when James Perrigo called for her, but she was about this morning and ready. The thing he offered her by way of amusement was not what she had been brought up to regard as pleasure, nor was it in any way related to those pleasures which had seemed so necessary to her during her life in New York City. Yet she looked forward to it with a curious anticipation. If one had asked her where she was going she might have answered that she was going slumming in the woods. Possibly there was something of that point of view, but there was more. There was curiosity, of course. But over and above these things was an eagerness which she herself did not understand, and which she resented vaguely. But eager she was.

James arrived in a battered car, suitable for such roads as they might have to follow in search of remote trout streams. In the tonneau were the tools of the fishing trade, materials for luncheon and a frying pan.

"Why the cooking utensil?" she asked as she got into the seat beside him.

"Trout," he answered sententiously.

"Get out of the wrong side of the bed?" she asked.

For a moment he did not appear to grasp her meaning, then he smiled. "Was I short?" he asked.

"Well, you didn't rush into a flood of details."

"I'd rather show you than talk about it. Why talk about a thing when you can do it? All set?"

"You may fire when ready, Gridley."

They drove in rather rickety fashion along the river, through the crisp tingle of early morning air, through odors of dew-touched vegetation and the tonic of spruce and balsam. It was clear, the green was a brilliant, freshly washed green, the sky seemed very lofty, and the voice of the river seemed somehow refreshed after the darkness. A mountain river has many voices, speaking together, but of all of them—if one will stop and listen until one singles it out—a silvery tinkle, as of strings of little bells, is the loveliest. It is always there, even when the stream is in torrent. But one must listen for it, separate it from the symphony and hold it apart. Curiously clear and distinct it is, and gracious and soothing.

A porcupine waddled across the roadway, reached the undergrowth, and there made as much tumult as would the passing of a black bear. Farther along, in a clearing, James pointed silently to a red fox, glorious tail extended, three feet on the ground, poised for that whisk which would transmute it into a vanishing flash of red. A mother partridge, taking a dust bath in a rut, ruffled her feathers and offered battle to the oncoming car. Sarah noted the darkening of James' eyes, the crinkling of their corners and the softening of his mouth as he slowed the car and turned out to save the bellicose matron from the consequences of a courage too great for her dimensions.

"It never offered to fly," she said in astonishment.

"Chicks back some place," he said, still sententious.

His eyes seemed to miss nothing; they watched the road to pick out the most comfortable passage, but, for all that, nothing in the bordering woods seemed to escape him. It was as if some extra sense informed him of the morning exhibits of the forests.

"Look!" He pointed upward to the low branch of a red maple; and Sarah, after peering eagerly, saw what seemed a tiny bunch of fur. But it was not fur; it was feathers. Three tiny owlets nestled together, the one in the middle erect, the two at the sides pressing close so that the three heads touched. There was something ludicrously bashful about their appearance as they stared down, big-eyed. They did not stir. James chuckled.

"Oh, weren't they"—she searched for a word and found it—"silly?" she said.

"Like three mountain children at a county fair," he said; and though she had never seen just that spectacle, she could imagine it, and laughed at the justness of his comparison. "Show me more."

He looked at her gravely. "This isn't the Bronx Zoo," he said. "They're not on exhibition in a line of cages." He shook his head. "I wouldn't like to see them that way."

"But millions of children who never would see them otherwise love the zoo."

"Maybe it's all right." For some minutes he drove silently, shaking his head as he considered Zoölogical gardens. "It's like picking a line of poetry out of its context," he said.

An eagle flew across their vision, a very distressed and hasty eagle, swinging and dodging and swerving, while above him a tiny dot flashed up and down furiously. The eagle uttered angry and apprehensive sounds. One could tell it wished itself some place else and wished it with all its heart.

"Kingbird," said James. "Their business is licking eagles. Pecking the stuffin' out of him." He chuckled again. "You can't see that in any zoo."

"The eagle was a hundred times bigger," Sarah said, astonished.

"You can afford to be a hundred times smaller— if you are a hundred times quicker," James said. "But what gets me is why a kingbird wants to pick on an eagle. What's his idea?"

"He probably hasn't any—and what does it matter?"

"What does anything matter?" James asked with a shrug. "I guess nothing really does. There isn't much difference in the importance of questions. Newton saw an apple fall and wanted to know why. I see a kingbird tackle an eagle and I want to know why. It wouldn't make much difference if neither of us found the answer. Gravity kept right on working after Newton solved it, and kingbirds will keep on tackling eagles."

"But the whole world uses gravity."

"Does it?" James asked. "And what of it?"

"You're a savage," she said smilingly.

"What's a savage? A savage is a fellow who isn't annoyed by civilization. Civilized folks call him a savage, and look down on him and are sorry for him or afraid of him. I bet he thinks a lot worse of the civilized ones."

"But we're right, and he's wrong."

"Who says so? Why, the civilized ones. Seems as though I'd rather be a savage, strolling along through the forest, than a civilized man in a Subway rush. Um—what do folks get out of civilization? In the last analysis, three meals a day, a roof, and clothes to satisfy the law; and Subway jams and sleeping cars and milk out of bottles and cold-storage eggs. The savage gets the three meals and the roof and what clothes he wants, without having to suffer hardships to get them."

"You forget the æsthetic side," said Sarah.

"Fiddlesticks! Your æsthetic things are artificial as a wooden leg. The only æsthetic things worth mentioning are emotions, and the savage has as many of them and uses them more. Art? Rats! Music has to be barbarous if it amounts to anything. Civilized music is bunk. . . . Literature? What novel can touch the word-of-mouth stories of the savage? They are in direct touch with their art—so it isn't art. It's part of the business of the day. We get our art secondhand, in an agreed set of symbols— and the symbols get to be the art instead of the substance."

"Gosh!" exclaimed Sarah. "You'd make a hit at a studio tea. Greenwich Village would give three rousing cheers for you. You're right up their street. Anything is that don't add up." Nevertheless, she was impressed, not so much by his philosophy as by the fact that he had one and could state it convincingly. It was the story of the trained cat—not that the cat could do such wonderful tricks, but that it was wonderful a cat could do any tricks at all! James owned a flashing mind—a mind which could hold its own among the intelligentsia of New York's round tables!

They came to a ramshackle covered bridge across the river, and there James stopped the car. "From here we walk," he said, slipping his arms through the strap of a pack and picking the rods from the car. "This bridge will hold us up, but I'd hate to put the weight of the car on it."

"How far?"

"Quite a piece. We'll follow the old tote road across to Checkerberry Brook. Kind of squashy walking in spots, maybe, but you had sense enough to wear something on your feet."

"You'd be surprised," she said, "to find out how much sense I have."

"I guessed it," he said. "You've got it—if you ever get around to use it."

"Of all things!"

"Think you can walk a trestle?"

"I never tried."

"Logging railroad used to run up beyond. Have to cross the still waters on the trestle—or wade."

They followed the narrow streak of grass which once had been a busy tote road upon whose iced bed great teams of steaming horses had dragged two-sled loads of logs. Bushes choked it; rocks protruded jaggedly, roots and stumps impeded the way.

"How ever did they drive over this?" Sarah asked.

"Three feet of ice and snow covered it. You could skate from here to town."

She was enjoying herself; she was happy—and it was not yet eight o'clock! She laughed at the absurdity of it.

They crossed the still waters on the rotting trestle; and then, leaving the road, cut up the hillside to circle around to the stream which fed that broad stretch of marsh and pool which made the flat almost impassable. There the stream regained its true nature, for, held tightly between granite banks, it tumbled and rushed and twittered and tinkled down little falls and miniature cataracts and rapids as it was meant to do. Fresh from its mountain springs the water was cold—cold enough to delight even the discriminating taste of the speckled trout.

They went on for perhaps a mile; and then,

swerving back to the brook again, commenced to fish
—that is, James fished while Sarah made strange
motions with her rod. Down and down they scram-
bled, James taking to the water, Sarah clinging pre-
cariously to the tumbled shore. The trout were not
large, but they were plentiful—and James seemed as
much in his natural element as they. She could not
but find him admirable. He was adroit, capable, sure
in his graceful movements, and undeniably handsome.

She wondered if he would be more handsome in
meticulously tailored clothes, or if something would
be lost; she tried to imagine him in drawing-rooms,
at studio teas, escorting her to the theater or to dance
afterward at noisy, smoky, promiscuous night clubs.
It was a picture which would not compose—and she
was glad of it. There was a satisfaction in the
thought that James would not fit into such a paint-
ing; that he would not care to fit into it. . . . On the
other hand she could see him, in his laced boots and
flannel shirt, and that air of his which mingled the
inscrutable with the charming, meeting the people she
knew and impressing them as he impressed her. He
would be unconscious that anything about himself
required amending; he would conduct himself with
dignity and without self-consciousness. In short,
Sarah was approaching the perilous conclusion that
James bulked larger than those men who previously
had been her ideal.

"It's noon," he said after a time. "Hungry?"

"Starved."

He nodded, settled his pack and creel on the ground and gathered bits of dry wood for a fire.

"Can I help?" she asked.

"Can you?" he asked, and smiled disarmingly. She was compelled to admit that she could not help —even with gathering the wood, though she tried. He was courteous about it, but she observed that the branches she brought to him invariably were discarded. And presently he had a little fire blazing, and the luncheon was spread. Deftly he opened the little fish, and the odor of them sizzling in bacon grease tantalized her appetite.

"After we eat," he said, "we'll catch you a mess to take home."

"Oh, maybe Warren could eat one!" she exclaimed.

"Your brother? Is he ——"

"Conscious since yesterday morning," she said, and then remembered that silence had been enjoined upon her. He eyed her curiously a moment, tapping meanwhile upon his knee with his fingers.

"Since yesterday morning! You didn't mention it."

"I ——"

"And news is pretty quick to get around Colchester."

"They thought best ——" she commenced lamely, and then fell awkwardly silent, because she did not know how to end her sentence.

James nodded slowly, as if with complete understanding, but for some moments he seemed distrait.

Suddenly she remembered Warren's injunction to step softly with this young man. Why? What had Warren in mind? For, she thought, it was unlike him to meddle in her social affairs—unlike him to meddle at all without reason. But what reason could there be? James was personable, of excellent if rural family, and wealthy. A distant rumble interrupted her thoughts, and she looked up, startled.

"Thunder?" she asked.

He nodded and turned to scrutinize the western sky; clouds were lifting there and he frowned. "Um —Camp 6 is nearest," he said half to himself. "We'd better make tracks or you'll get soaked."

"What's Camp 6?"

"Old set of logging buildings down past the still waters," he said. "But there'll be a roof and walls, and probably an old stove." As he spoke he was busily stowing things in his pack. "Come on," he said boylike, and she followed him as, glancing about him an instant to get his direction, he cut across country toward his destination. There was something efficient in that; no pausing, no wondering where he was or which would be the quickest way. One glance and he knew.

The clouds built themselves rapidly into black, boiling masses, and thunder rolled continuously; she gathered from his face that, in spite of the danger of a wetting, he liked it; he liked the menace of the sky and the reverberations of the thunder between the hills. She should have been afraid, but she was not

afraid; he inspired confidence. It was as if he knew
all about storms, and particularly about this one, and
saw nothing in it to excite alarm. Far across the
valley she could see the gray bank that meant falling
rain, and he adjured her to hasten.

Now they were at the abandoned railway, leaping
from rotting tie to rotting tie.

"Look out for your ankles," he cautioned her.
And then, as if as an afterthought: "Folks go lame
in the woods from stepping on branches and logs.
Always step over if you can; it's better. But never
step on one with your instep; always with the toe.
I've seen greenhorns so lame they couldn't walk."

Presently he turned off to the left up an incline,
and there she saw, sprawling before her, the slat-
ternly bulk of the set of camps, the hovel for the
horses, the cookhouse, the bunk house, the scaler's
shanty. The hovel and scaler's shanty were of logs,
the others of boards; and all showed upon their roofs
the remnants of the tar paper which once had made
them tight against the weather.

"The cook shanty looks best," said James. "That
roof's hung on."

He strode to the door and wrenched it open, standing back for her to enter. She saw before her a
huge room, low-roofed. The light was dim, but she
made out a long table down one side, a couple of
bunks constructed from spruce saplings on the other,
and at the far end a stove. And then she drew a
sudden breath, for there was a fire in the stove.

Quickly she drew to one side to allow James to enter.

"There's a fire," she whispered.

James strode into the room and glanced about. Clearly, he found nothing alarming in a fire; it meant to him that some fisherman or hunter or woodsman had taken shelter in the building just as they had, and he advanced into the room with Sarah at his side. Then, out of a shadowy corner a figure reared itself, features indistinguishable, but even in that dim light seen to be of great bulk.

"Hello," said James. "How's chances?" The greeting of the lumber camps.

"I knew," said the man in a snarling voice, "if anybody come snoopin' around it 'ud be you."

The man advanced toward them, brushed past them rudely, slammed shut the door and dropped the bar into place. There he stood, crouching and scowling and working his mouth.

"Latzo!" said James softly, half to himself.

Sarah clutched his arm, for suddenly she had become very much afraid.

CHAPTER XXI

JAMES slipped the pack from his back and tossed it upon the long table. Sarah pressed close to him as if for protection, and he shook his head and smiled at her.

"Stand over there, Sarah," he said, pointing. "Keep out from underfoot." Then to Latzo: "I told you to clear out of the country."

"There's a difference between bein' told and doin'," said the man, and showed his teeth in a grin. "He kind of hoped you'd come nosin' in here. He's got it all fixed so's you won't be missed serious. Looks like he's ambitious to be the only Perrigo the' is."

James continued to look at Latzo, but spoke to Sarah. "When this fracas starts," he said, "you open that door and hiper for town, storm or no storm. Follow the old railroad."

She did not answer, but stared, terrified, at the lowering, unshaven, bestial face of the man who crouched before the door. He appeared monstrous, immensely powerful. His great hands hung almost to his knees, his shoulders and thighs were colossal and his mat of unkempt hair magnified the circumference of his round head. She watched, fascinated, as he crouched lower, saw his frame quiver and knit beneath his rough clothing, saw the dull fire glow in his close-set eyes. It seemed to her that James, erect, was not so tall as Latzo, crouched; a lad facing a full-grown man. James stood slender, almost slight in her apprehensive eyes, which sought his face and were astonished to see it wear a grave speculative smile. A crackling flash of lightning followed instantly by an ear-splitting smash of thunder made her cower; the cook shanty quivered. She was aware that Latzo moved, slid forward one huge foot along the boards, then the other, a slow advance, with something inexorably malign in the movement. She wanted to scream.

There was a scurry over the boards; two figures stood where Latzo's had been alone, and the vicious spat of blows reached her ears. James had not awaited Latzo's elephantine rush, but himself, swiftly, disconcertingly, had taken the initiative. Three times he struck from the shoulder with all the power of his slender, wiry body—and was out of reach before the man, straightened out of his crouch, could regain balance to lash out at him in retaliation. Sarah uttered a little cry and clasped her hands upon her breast. Kingbird and eagle! Kingbird and eagle!

"When he leaves the door—git!" James said to her.

She saw Latzo straighten suddenly and lash out with his calked shoe at James' kneecap, but James was inside, struck again while the man was off balance, and he went to the floor. James stepped back and waited, but it was no mistaken chivalry which animated him; it was caution, the working of a quick intelligence. For he knew that if he were to survive, it must be by quickness of mind and quickness of body. Latzo was a fighter of lumber camps and bar-rooms, more at home when rolling on the floor than on his feet; a gouger of eyes, a thruster of knees, a user of teeth. Once permit Latzo's hand to close upon his ankle and there was the end of it. Nor did he draw false satisfaction from the illusion that such blows as he had struck could win for him quickly —or at all. Such battering the man could endure for hours and remain dangerous; would suffer it willingly if at last he might lay clutching hand upon his adversary and drag him into a back-breaking hug. So James fought to cut, to blind. If he could but close Latzo's eyes, things might go well.

Latzo got to his knees, to his feet, and lurched forward with body bent and arms spread wide; not again did he rush, but shuffled forward slowly, slowly, little eyes glowing, blood trickling from the pulp which had been his lips. To force James back and ever backward—that was his necessity—back and back until the young man's shoulder touched the wall—until he should be cornered, left without space in which to dart in and out, to strike and avoid. Then, when there could be no more retreat, Latzo would press in regardless of what punishment he received; he could take it—take all James had to offer—if he could but come to grips, breast to breast.

James gave back purposely to draw Latzo from the door. But Sarah did not move, even when the way was clear; she could not have moved. She was fascinated, but something more than fascinated. An emotion arose within her which she did not comprehend; there was terror in it, but there was also joy. It was a primitive emotion such as New York could never have given her, a mingling of pride, of excitement, of loyalty, deriving from those days when men lived in caves and fought for their women with teeth and with club. She could not go. And at the end of it she knew the real reason why she could not go was because she could not desert her man in his hour of danger!

Toward the opposite wall James was being pressed foot by foot; then, feinting to the right, he leaped to the left, brushed the table with his back and reversed the field of battle. Again he essayed the feat, but the table was too close. Sarah cried out as it impeded him, saw him rest his right hand upon its top and vault sidewise and rearward until he stood in the narrow space behind with the table between him and Latzo, and, before the man could reach the table's edge, James set his hands against it and heaved. Latzo stumbled back as the length of boards crashed at his feet, and again James was at him—kingbird upon eagle—sending him teetering to his heels with clean, swift, well-timed blows. Latzo wrapped his face in his arms, bellowing, and rushed headlong.

Now he launched great swinging blows, again driving James back and ever backward. Lightning flashed, thunder reverberated, but none in that cook shanty were conscious of the severity of the storm. Not all Latzo's blows were missing; James did not escape scot-free; and one of them, only one, if it struck home squarely upon a vulnerable spot, would lift James from his feet, unconscious, helpless. One of Latzo's eyes was closed; his face had assumed new proportions, but the enormous animal vitality of the man had not been sapped. His strength remained, his vindictive determination was unweakened.

Speed against strength! If one be a hundred times swifter, one may be a hundred times less powerful. Again and again Sarah thought of that as she watched, spellbound. James was swift—swift and sure—and fearless. That she could sense, and something more—that he rejoiced in it. Whatever the outcome he was living now. At times his face was amused, at others alight with such a fire as one must associate with creative inspiration. He was creating; instead of writing his epic, he was living it!

It could not continue; either speed must flag under the weight of exhaustion, or brute strength must ebb under constant battering. James seemed to feel something of this, for, with a sudden calculated swirl, he launched himself upon Latzo, in and out, striking, whipping in blows, dancing away, never set, but always poised. And his objective was that other eye. Latzo gave ground; for the first time he gave ground; for the first time he seemed to feel respect for his antagonist. He darted glances about the room with the open eye which remained to him, and then began backing, shifting, working his way to an objective. Toward the back of the room he allowed himself to be driven until the stove was close behind him; then, uttering a savage howl, he stopped his retreat and threw himself into a lumbering, lunging, dangerous offensive. James gave back before the flurry, and that was as Latzo desired it, for it gave him an instant of time, the instant he required to crouch, snatch at the helve of the ax with which he had chopped his firewood.

Sarah screamed. James leaped, kicked at the gnarled fingers which clutched the hickory, but failed to tear them loose. But as the man surged upward there was time for one blow—one swift, timed, savage jab—and Latzo staggered back, ax lifted before him, but unable to see his enemy. For James had found his opening. His left fist, driven by all the weight and leverage of his splendid body, had crashed against that seeing eye—and Latzo was blinded!

The man stood, spitting evil language, lashing about him at the enemy he could not see. The ax swished through the air, swished again and again. James poised on his toes, just out of reach, waiting, eyes level, steady, but eager and joyous. Latzo kept the weapon in play. James smiled and scraped his feet on the floor. He reached for and seized quietly a pan from off the stove and tossed it to the floor at Latzo's left, so that the man spun toward the sound and swung his ax hopefully. And James was ready; as that swing of the ax turned the man half around, half away, James rooted his feet to the floor, set himself so that every ounce of his weight and power could be delivered with the blow, and struck. Once he struck, his knuckles falling just below Latzo's ear. The man's arms dropped and he sagged. Twice he struck, and Latzo's knees buckled. Three times he struck—and it was the end. Power departed from Latzo, and consciousness departed, and he lay grotesquely with face ground against the floor.

Something welled up within Sarah Cross which was not relief; it was more splendid, more glorious than relief. It was pride—tremendous, sudden-blazing pride. He had won—and how he had won!

She rejoiced in him; cried out in the savage yet tender glory of her rejoicing: "James! James!"

He turned, smiled, shook his head and took two steps to the bench, upon which he dropped. And she was at his side, kneeling at his feet. "James!"

"You didn't go," he said, and his eyes glowed.

"Go! And leave you?"

He took her face between his bruised and battered hands, nor did she shrink, and he bent closer to scrutinize her, to read her soul, and then, whatever of grimness had hardened his face, whatever of battle lust or savagery, vanished to be replaced by a glow of gentleness, of happiness.

"Then," he asked, "it's all right?"

"Oh, so very, very all right!" she whispered.

He touched her cheek, brushed back her hair and then lifted her to her feet. "We've a lifetime for this," he said, and bent over Latzo. The man did not move. James stood erect and peered about the room; in the corner he saw standing a trunk—a small flat trunk.

"So that ———" he said softly.

"James, James, what does it mean? What is it all about? Why did he attack you?"

He smiled as he answered, but it was a crooked, mirthless smile. "Just a family affair," he said.

The storm was passing; thunder receded into the distance; presently the sun would break through to turn the forest into a refreshed paradise of glistening green. James threw open the door and looked outside.

"You'll have to carry the fish," he said gravely. "I've got other business. The wet won't hurt us—and we'd better make time."

He swung the trunk to his shoulder and stepped out into the muddy way.

"What's that? What do you want of the man's trunk?" Sarah asked.

"There's nothing in the world I want less than this trunk," he said gravely, "but it's got to come."

He paused a moment. "You meant it when you said it was all right?"

"Yes, dear," she said.

"You may change your mind," he said gloomily.

"Change my mind! Why? When?"

"Well," he said, "when this trunk gets to town—among other things. But maybe I can pull it off." This last was to himself.

"Pull what off, James?"

He shook his head. "The house is tumbling down," he said cryptically.

"Let it tumble—let everything tumble—who cares?" Then her mind swiftly veered. "James, why wouldn't Eunice see me when I called? Didn't she want this to happen—you and me?"

He spoke very gravely now. "Eunice is all right," he said. "Remember that. Remember I told you that. No matter what happens, Perrigo blood or not, Eunice is all right."

"What a strange thing to say!"

"Strange things must be said after strange things have been done," he said, and swung into his stride down the muddy road. Even though he carried a burden on his shoulders Sarah found it not easy to keep pace with him.

At last they reached the covered bridge and the car. James lowered the trunk into the tonneau, helped Sarah to her seat, and himself took the wheel. Presently he spoke. "Let us not talk," he said. "We must leave things where they are—until tomorrow.

Then we can—then you can take them up again if—
if you still want to."

"What do you mean, James? You're so strange."
She flushed and then grew pale. "Do you mean—
have I—was I wrong, James, and you—you don't
want me after all?"

"Don't be a little fool," James said, which, although it was undeniably brusque and rude to a
degree, seemed for some reason to be perfectly satisfactory to Sarah.

An hour later the car stopped before her door.
James got down, helped her to alight and dragged
out the trunk.

"This goes in your house," he said.

"What?"

"In your house." He turned his level brown eyes
upon her. "And you're to keep still about it," he
said.

"Yes, sir; thank you, sir," Sarah said with make-
believe meekness—which covered a meekness which
was very real, indeed.

CHAPTER XXII

KNUCKLES arose with the intention of precipitating matters. He went first to the post office, where he found in his box a letter bearing the return address of the firm of lawyers in Boston whom he had intrusted with the work of investigating the People's Lumber Company. This he thrust unopened into his pocket, deeming it best to give it his attention in private; after which he climbed into his car with the flapping mud guards and drove to the mill. Two hours before he passed Warren Cross' house, James and Sarah had started upon their fishing excursion; they were now across the covered bridge and approaching the stream which was their objective.

He pushed open the office door and nodded to the girl at the adjoining desk. "Where's Walter?" he asked.

"Out of town. I guess he drove, because I was up to the train. The word we got was that he prob'ly wouldn't be back before tomorrow night, maybe."

"Know where he went?"

"He didn't say."

This was rather an impasse. One could not function upon an absent individual. But there was James —he might be utilized as a substitute.

"Where's James?" he asked.

"Nobody ever knows where James is."

If Knuckles was disappointed it did not disclose itself on his wind-tanned face. He went back to his car and drove toward the village, hesitating as he passed the Cross house, but thinking better of the impulse to stop and continuing on his way. Then he remembered the letter, and drawing up to the roadside ran his thumb nail under the flap of the envelope. The report was lengthy, and from the manner in which Knuckles' eyes narrowed, evidently not to his liking. Its disclosures, innocent enough if removed from their context, were quite enough to surprise; in fact, they were upsetting.

Walter Perrigo's name did not appear upon those typewritten sheets. Walter had nothing whatever to do with the People's Lumber Company, even to the ownership of a share of stock! But James Perrigo's name did appear. James, in short, owned the People's Lumber Company. This enterprise, devised for the purpose of defrauding the Colchester mill, belonged to James, lock, stock and barrel!

Knuckles did not like it; it challenged his intelligence and derided his reasoning powers. Yet it was in keeping with the evidence which, day by day, had been piling up under his hand. James, James—always James. And with this disclosure the last tangible thread connecting Walter with anything of a nefarious nature was severed.

But Knuckles was not satisfied; it was stubbornness. From the beginning he had known Walter to be in it. The idea never had occurred to him that possibly Walter might be exactly what he seemed—a middle-aged, rather bald, round-faced, unsociable incompetent. And though he had played with the notion that James might be the directing mind, he had doubted it. But that James and James alone was the malign agent he had not even imagined.

James! James had been on the scene when Warren Cross was injured. James had sent Latzo away, obviously to remove from the scene an accomplice who might become a witness. James this and James that—and now James was the sole owner of the People's Lumber Company. It meant a complete revision of Knuckles' plans and estimates, and a fresh commencement along a new road of attack. Knuckles was disappointed. He had wanted to get Walter; even though James was a Perrigo, he had not been personally offensive. Knuckles, in his dry way, had rather approved of James. And James, if he were as the facts seemed to show him, was to Knuckles' mind a dozen times more dangerous than Walter. Walter might cower and shrink from some overt act; James was a cat of another color.

He drove on into town and, as he passed the bank, an idea occurred to him. It was a thousand-to-one chance, but why not go in and see? He walked to the window behind which Henry Bridge was wont to face the world and nodded. "Mornin', Henry."

"Mornin', Ab."

"Busy?"

"Not's you could notice. I'm gettin' thin eatin' to the hotel. Kitty's livin' most of the time up to Crosses'."

"Hear any news of him? How's he makin' it?"

"Kitty's kind of encouraged, seems as though."

"Um—Aunt Hat there yet?"

"Try and drive her away," said Henry. "Gosh, I hope it turns out all right! I downright liked that feller. Yes, sir, I liked him. Hope this don't take him away from town."

"His wife don't act like Colchester was the apple of her eye."

"Oh, wimmin!" said Henry. "Mis' Cross is all right as soon's she catches on to us. You watch."

"Hope so. . . . Happen to know a man by the name of Latzo?"

"Uh-huh. Works down to the mill. Cashes his pay checks here. Sure I remember him. He——" Henry bit off the end of that sentence and glanced sharply at Knuckles.

"He what?" Knuckles said.

"Interested in him special?"

"Extry special," said Knuckles.

"Business deal?"

"Kind of."

"Wa-al"—Henry's voice was hesitant—"I dunno's there's any harm sayin'. He hain't a depositor."

" 'N' he won't be," said Knuckles.

"It kind of surprised me, him a laborin' man and all."

"What surprised you, Henry?"

"Why, him cashin' a big check."

"Cashed it here, did he?" Knuckles said, pretending to more knowledge than he had.

"Thousand dollars, it was. He took it in hundreds."

"Call to mind whose check it was?"

"That was a kind of a surprise too. Didn't know he had anythin' to do with a business in Boston."

"Didn't you? People's Lumber Company, wan't it?"

"Looks like you know," said Henry.

"And signed by James Perrigo?"

"Yeah—James."

"Um—got it yet?"

"Might have. We ain't always as prompt sendin' through as city banks. If it didn't go down last night, we got it."

"Look," said Knuckles.

Henry investigated, returning presently with a canceled check in his hands. "There she be."

Knuckles nodded. "Hang on to it, Henry. I'll be responsible. Satisfact'ry?"

"What's goin' on, Ab?"

"Friend of Cross', hain't you?"

"Yes."

"Then keep that check locked up where you can lay hands on it."

" 'Tain't bankin'," said Henry.

"What," demanded Knuckles, "is a little bankin' between friends?"

"I'll go you—once," Henry said, "if I never see the back of my neck."

Knuckles went out to his car, but before he got in he paused, frowned and kicked the running board. "Dog-gone!" he said under his breath.

He had recollected the events of the night before. Why, in view of all this evidence piling up against James, had Latzo sneaked out of concealment to carry away a trunk for Walter? And what was in the trunk?

Knuckles did not enter his car, but swung across the street to his father's office. The old squire was alone. The young man sprawled in a chair and tapped on his knee with sinewy fingers.

"I don't know but what I'm flummoxed," he said.

"Time you was less headstrong," said the old gentleman through lips which scarcely moved. "Lately you been gittin' too big for your bigness."

"I'm sizin' down this mornin'. . . . Mebby you can make head or tail out of this."

He marshaled his facts while the old justice listened impassively, making no comment until the end: "So, seems as though, Walter hain't in it and James's got both feet in the trough."

"Looks so."

"Um—I been a-listenin' to evidence all my life, and weighin' it and jedgin' the credibility of witnesses. The's times when you got to look deeper'n witnesses and oaths and what kin be seen with the eye."

"Mebby," said Knuckles.

"If this here James was sent to the penitentiary," said the old man, "Walter wouldn't suffer none by it." Knuckles looked up quickly. "Walter'd have the handlin' of James' share," said his father. "Um —dunno's I'd jump to no conclusions so early in the mornin'. The way you got things sized up, they turn out better for Walter than any other you kin think up."

"Yes," said Knuckles.

The old man cleared his throat. "The Young Doc's a all-fired talkative feller," said the justice, changing the subject. "Seems like he's cal'latin' to git folks down on him. Uh-huh. Kind of overestimates cases, seems as though. Allus implyin' he was jest called in the nick of time. Blows his own horn consid'able." Knuckles nodded. He was not interested in the Young Doc. "Goes around displayin' how much he knows," said Mr. Knuckles, "and if he hain't careful he'll use it all up some mornin' and have nothin' to gas about afternoons."

"Folks say he's smart."

"He cal'lates to be," Mr. Knuckles said dryly. "I heard him holdin' forth las' night. Him and a few was a-standin' out there, spittin' and swappin' stories, and then Young Doc he got the floor and give quite a talk. Walter Perrigo was amongst 'em."

Knuckles straightened up with sudden interest.

"It sounded like the Doc was volunteerin' information, but the way I heard it, it was led up to. Kind of a word pushed in here and another shoved in there. Primin' the pump, like. They started off talkin' about how to set a fractured leg, and that somehow led 'em on to morphine to quiet the pain. Young Doc was mighty interestin' on morphine."

Knuckles nodded.

"And then," said the squire, "he got to discoursin' on other drugs and sich-like, till he come to strychnine. Seems like he knows all about strychnine. Different ones asked him questions."

"I bet you," said Knuckles.

"And one question kind of led up to another, and so on. And in the end the Young Doc was gittin' right down to how much and how often. Yes, sir, he killed off cats and he killed off skunks and he killed off hosses. Kind of a slaughterin' mood. He got most interestin', though, when he got around to not killin' off. Somehow he was got to describe jest how much a body'd have to take to make him tarnation sick, but so's he'd git over it."

"Who asked that question?" Knuckles wanted to know.

" 'Twan't Walter," said the justice; "but Walter he asked one a couple of questions back that led up to it."

"It ain't evidence," said Knuckles.

"But," said the old man, "it's illuminatin'. I got to supposin'. And I supposed what if two folks was p'isoned side by side, out of the same dish, as you might say. And one of 'em died of it, but the other got well after consid'able of an effort. Um—'tain't in nature to suspect a body of p'isonin' himself."

"No, don't seem so."

"But if the' was a third one there, and he didn't git p'isoned or anything, he'd have to do consid'able explainin'. And if the' was other damagin' facts to come out on top of it——"

"Con-sarn!" exclaimed Knuckles.

"And then," said Mr. Knuckles, "one 'ud be dead and one in the penitentiary for life—and one down with a stummick ache. But when he got up ag'in and his stummick didn't gripe no more, he'd be what the' was left, wouldn't he?"

"Anybody can get strychnine," said Knuckles.

"The conclusion I come to," said the old man dryly, "is that young men hain't allus smarter'n their fathers."

"I came here, didn't I?"

"Might 'a' come sooner with profit. . . . And another conclusion I come to was that if I was a young feller and would ruther go to her weddin' than her funeral, I'd take steps."

"I cal'late to," said Knuckles.

"I been considerin' her—and things," said the squire. Knuckles paused in the door and turned his head. "And the's times," went on his father, "when a body has to revise his notions."

Knuckles understood, and was relieved. The subject of Eunice Perrigo never would be brought up between them again, no matter how things turned out. But, by some process of reasoning, Eunice had been absolved of the crime of possessing Perrigo blood.

CHAPTER XXIII

WALTER PERRIGO returned from New York—he had been in New York—by taking a train to the little city twenty miles away and by driving thence to Colchester in his car. He was well satisfied with himself, for the end of his labors was in view—a gratifyingly successful end. He had met with Mr. Woodson of the Consolidated Lumber Corporation, and then with the assembled board of directors. To them he had made his proposition—a proposition advantageous to one who had sold a mill for an excellent price and would buy it back at one less excellent. But it is the modern method of business to minimize losses. These astute gentlemen of the board considered it cheaper to take a moderate loss in a lump than to hang on with the prospect of meeting with a string of annual deficits. The matter was closed, Walter paid a substantial sum to bind the bargain, and now was returning to Colchester to await the drafting of the final papers of transfer.

"What about Cross?" Woodson had asked the board.

"Tell him not to worry. No blame attaches to him. His old position will be waiting for him when he is able to take it. Will you give him that assurance, Mr. Perrigo?"

"It will be a pleasure," said Walter.

Now he was almost at home again. One more step remained to complete his success, and that step must be taken at once. He had no doubt of its efficacy or apprehension of danger to himself. And then he, and he alone, would be in possession of the Perrigo fortune, and the world would be his oyster. Another twelve hours—another eight hours, possibly—and the thing would be done!

He drove his car into the garage, entered the house, announced his presence to the housekeeper and went to his room. Presently the supper bell rang, and he went down at the dining room, where James already sat at table. Walter nodded, peered at James' hands, which were thickly bandaged, and drawing up his chair asked, "What you been doing to yourself?"

"Skinned my knuckles," said James.

The housekeeper came in with steaming soup. Walter spoke to her. "Fix up a tray for Eunice," he said; "I'll take it up. Haven't seen her since I came in. How is she?" he asked casually, turning to James.

James shrugged his shoulders in answer and applied himself to his dish. The doorbell rang and the housekeeper answered. In a moment she appeared, flustered, in the dining-room door with Knuckles at her heels.

"He come right in," she said. "He jest pushed right in."

"Wanted to be sure of gettin' in," said Knuckles.

"Now that you are in, what d'ye want?" Walter asked shortly.

"Wanted to see you. Waited till you got back. Come right up so's time wouldn't be lost."

"What's your business?" Walter demanded.

"Go right ahead and eat. I'll talk while you're eatin'." He pulled a chair to the table, and sat, leaning his elbows on the cloth. Walter glowered, James eyed him passively.

"It's about the mill," said Knuckles.

"What about the mill? I don't see as the mill's any of your affair."

"I cal'late to tell you—you hold your horses," said Knuckles. "Don't let me upset your appetite."

The pantry door opened and the housekeeper appeared with a tray, advancing to Walter's chair. "Here's Eunice's supper," she said. Walter hesitated the fraction of a second, then arose and took it from her. Omitting the graciousness of asking to be excused he stepped to and through the door and disappeared into the hall. Knuckles stiffened, sat erect, then leaped to his feet and followed. James did not stir; he appeared not to be interested.

At the foot of the curved stairway Knuckles overtook Walter. "I'm in a hurry," he said. "I cal'late Eunice can wait a few minutes."

Walter halted, his eyes furtive, and made as if to push his way upward. Knuckles reached out and lifted the tray from Walter's hands, the sheer surprise of the man making it possible.

"You can take this up after a while," Knuckles said, and returned to the dining room, where he placed the tray within arm's reach, quietly seating himself again. Walter blustered.

"You get to thunder out of here," he said. "Coming into a man's house and snatching trays out of his hands! For a cent we'd throw you out on your ear." He looked to James for support, but James seemed to be paying no attention whatever. "Say your say and get out," Walter finished lamely.

"I'm in charge down to the mill," Knuckles said.

"What?"

"There's my authority," Knuckles said, tossing across the paper. Walter read it and sneered.

"Not much good," he said.

"It'll do till something better turns up. And so I came up to talk things over and see if maybe we couldn't get to the root. I don't want to take any unwarranted action."

"Such as?" Walter demanded, feeling the ground more secure under his feet.

"You and James getting through," said Knuckles.

Walter smiled unpleasantly. "I cal'late to do what hiring and firing is done," he said. "Cross doesn't count—not now. I bought the mill last night. The deal's closed."

"Um—mebby," said Knuckles. "Anyhow we got

to talk. There's the People's Lumber Company in Boston."

"What's that?"

"I wondered if you knew. It's a company that James owns. Retail lumber. Uh-huh. James holds all the stock in his name."

"What's this?" Walter said, swinging to his brother; but James continued to address himself to his soup.

"You ran high to Number 3 Common," said Knuckles. "We kind of got to the reason for it. The mill was shipping prime stuff to James' company and billing it as low-grade. Kind of profitable, seems as though."

Walter frowned; he frowned at James. "You imply that my brother has been ——"

"——swindlin' the company. Looks so, Walter. . . . And then Cross got hurt. Kind of timely. Just after he'd discharged you. And James was right on the spot, and Latzo was on top of the pile. And then Latzo up and disappears after James has a talk with him. Makes things look black for James."

"James —— You can't get away with this kind of talk, Knuckles. I know you and your father hate us. Don't sit there like a bump on a log, James, and let him practically accuse you of—trying to kill Cross."

"Better listen, I guess," James said imperturbably.

"Then there was the check—signed with James'

ur mother's side,"
ell she was a fine woman."
die," said James.

e's stopped from doing more."
"Yes."

name—that paid Latzo for whatever it paid him for.
A thousand dollars."

Walter was staring at his brother now—staring
at him and drawing back from him a little. "James
—you didn't—this is a pack of lies, isn't it? Say
something. Can't you say something?"

"Not to speak of," said James.

"You—you're not admitting it!"

"Let's keep on listenin'," said James.

"It looks pretty black for James," Knuckles said,
"but I got to have it made clear James was in it
alone."

"You don't imply that I——"

"I don't imply anythin'—only I was wonderin'
why folks in Boston, when they were shown James'
picture, didn't recognize him—even folks in his own
office. And why, when they were shown your picture,
they kept on insistin' it was James."

Walter gripped the arms of his chair; his eyes
glowed now with an unpleasant fire; his round cheeks
seemed suddenly to have lost their rotundity and to
have taken on an unsightly color between white and
gray.

"Which," said Knuckles, "would make that check
to Latzo from the People's Lumber Company come
from you, and not James."

Knuckles glanced at James now; that young man's
brown eyes were dark now, and troubled; but there
was no alarm in them, only something which seemed
to Knuckles like grief.

make r

"Pretty bad,"

"But the last isn't goi
aren't going to be poisoned—not while
reach of this tray. You can eat your o
you got appetite for it, Walter, but I cal'late
this tray by me till the chemist finds strychnine in it
And that's that. What you cal'late to do, Walter?"

"If," said Knuckles, "James got convicted of somethin' and sent off, you 'n' Eunice would be all the' was left. But Eunice made one too many, even then."

"You—you're crazy. I don't know what James has done, but I—you can't——"

"Wa-al," said Knuckles, "I can prove what you egged the Young Doc to talk about t'other night. I can prove how interested you was in poison."

James drew a breath and leaned sharply forward.

"I can prove you was curious to find out how much would kill a person, and how much another person could take—and come through alive. . . . Listenin', James? Seems as though you ought to."

"I'm listening."

"Now if three folks are in a house, and two of 'em are poisoned, and one dies and one gets well, why, it's the third one gets suspected. Wouldn't you say so?"

"I would say so," said James gravely.

"And if there was outside evidence he was a crook, and tried to kill Warren Cross, and all, it would ⠀t look bad for him."

" said James.

⠀ing to happen. Two folks
⠀ ⠀ I keep within
⠀ ⠀wn dish if
⠀ ⠀o keep

Walter sat mouthing, glaring, gripping the arms of his chair in a terror that made him voiceless. The thing had come too suddenly, been too complete; and where solid ground had sustained him, now opened a bottomless abyss. He made sounds.

James leaned across the table. "Officer of the law?" he asked.

"No," said Knuckles.

"Killing a man," said James, "isn't the worst crime—even poisoning. Stealing and cheating—they hardly seem to count. But it's pretty bad when a brother goes to lay such crimes on a brother—and just for money." Knuckles was silent. "But, just the same, he's my brother—half of him. He's got the same name. And it would be sort of terrible for a girl—having folks know she had that kind of a brother."

"Seems as though," said Knuckles.

"You got to the finish of it before I did," said James. "But I had double work. It was almost more than anybody could manage to undo what he did—and protect him too. I couldn't give up my brother, could I?"

"I cal'late you get it from yo███ said Knuckles. "I hear t███

"Cross won███

"No."

"H█

"Then what'll satisfy you? Seeing you're no sworn officer of the law ——"

"Stoppin' ain't enough. He's got to give back."

"I'll see to that."

"Seems like he ought to be punished some."

"What if he was to be given a night of time—till morning, say—and a thousand dollars to help him on his way? Walter loves money. Having none will be a sore hurt."

"There's the mill," said Knuckles.

"He will assign the papers to you."

"Kind of in trust till we look around," said Knuckles.

"And he wouldn't come back—or use our name— or make himself remembered to us—ever. That would have to be part of it. Does it satisfy you?"

"I'm satisfied."

James leaned across the table. "Walter," he said in a quiet voice, but one which Knuckles never would forget, "you are going away. You are going to do all I have said. You are never coming back. Not for fear of the law, Walter, but for fear of me. I've endured past enduring. If ever you set foot within a hundred miles of me, or write me, or let me hear of you—then I'll find you, Walter, and, brother or no brother, I'll kill you with my hands."

Walter glanced from one to the other wolfishly. It was the end; he was caught and there was no escape; but it was better than he had dared to hope —better than they knew. Money! He sneered an

inward, secret sneer. Turn him loose in the world
with no name and a thousand dollars to see him on
his way! He gritted his teeth to hold back the ela-
tion which might have sown suspicion had it appeared on his face. . . . They didn't know! The
trunk—the trunk Latzo guarded—ignorant of its
content. And its content was a fortune in untrace-
able currency.

He struggled to his feet. "Then—I can go?" he
said with difficulty.

What must be done by way of signing and signa-
tures was completed. Walter moved toward the door.
James turned his back and stared through a window
at the blackness of the night.

"I suppose," Walter said, unable to keep a sneer
from his voice, "I can have my own car to travel in."

"Take everything," James said without turning,
"which will remind us you ever lived."

When James faced the room again Walter was
gone. Knuckles stood staring at the floor, nor did
he lift his eyes as James stepped toward him and
touched his arm.

"We're obliged—Eunice and I," he said. That
was all.

As for Walter, he backed out his car, and driving
recklessly as he had never driven before, as it had
never been in him to drive, he sped to the covered
bridge. There he took to his feet and stumbled
through the darkness of the forest for what seemed
to him torturing, interminable hours, until he

breasted the hill upon which stood abandoned Camp 6. Panting and exhausted he threw open the door and called, "Latzo! Latzo!"

The lumberjack stirred in his bunk, rolled savagely to his feet and struck a light. "What you doin' here?"

"I came for my trunk. I've got to go away. Help me to the car with my trunk."

"Huh! Kind of a hurry!" Latzo held the lamp so it shone upon Walter's features, and needed no man to tell him Walter was a fugitive, hunted, bewildered. "They ketched ye, eh? And you and your trunk! Wa-al, I got money comin'. If you're runnin' I got to run too."

"You'll get yours when we make the car. It's there. Where's the trunk?"

"There hain't no trunk," said Latzo.

"What?" The word was shrill, almost a screech. Walter clawed at Latzo's arm.

"Look me over," Latzo said. "Think I look this way nat'ral? That wildcat brother of yourn done it —and he's got the trunk."

Reason departed from Walter; he mouthed and cursed; he clawed at Latzo, who pushed him off with a snarl; he uttered words which would better have been left unuttered, and among them were these:

"They cheated me! James knew—and he sent me off with a thousand dollars—to live, and with a thousand dollars! Every cent! Me—with a thousand dollars!" He laughed terribly and slapped his pocket. "A thousand dollars!"

Latzo blinked. "Thousand dollars, eh? Better'n a b'ile on the neck." And he grinned.

It might have been fifteen minutes later when the man Latzo came out of the door; dawn was beginning to break in the east. There was sufficient light so that he could pause to count the roll of bills which his hand clutched. A thousand dollars! He turned away to the southward, beating into the woods which he was well able to traverse, and vanished.

No second man came through the door. . . . Dawn became morning and morning became noon— and the door did not open. Night descended, and it was very still, dreadfully still.

CHAPTER XXIV

JAMES and Knuckles stood in the dining room, nor did they speak again until the sound of Walter's car had disappeared in the distance. Then Knuckles lifted his eyes. "Eunice," he said.

"Upstairs," said James. "Her disposition ain't so good. No. Too kind of reckless, she was, and she'd found out something, and—we just had to keep her quiet."

"I wouldn't have been so uneasy," Knuckles said, "if I'd known about you."

James shot a quick glance at Knuckles' face. "Uneasy?" he asked.

Knuckles returned the look directly. "I want Eunice," he said. "Object?"

"No," said James. And then: "I hated to do it—she don't forgive easily—but I couldn't have her running around."

"She'd have told me what she knew—next time," said Knuckles.

"I'll tell you tomorrow," James said. "What she knew is at the Cross house. I'll come there at nine; there's things to arrange. . . . Want to see Eunice?"

"Hain't ready—yet," said Knuckles. "Night."

At nine o'clock they met in the Cross parlor.

James had arrived first and was in significant talk with Sarah when Knuckles arrived. She spoke to Knuckles, let her hand brush James' shoulder as she stood up and left the room, and Knuckles smiled comprehendingly.

"Um," he said.

"That was on my mind, too," James said. "Kind of crowded, seems as though. . . . I put it in the hall closet. Just a moment."

He appeared presently bearing the little trunk. "Eunice saw into this—that's why," he said. "Walter took the keys. We'll have to pry it open."

It was accomplished with as little sound as possible, and Knuckles stood with puckered brow, looking down at the contents.

"How's this fit in?"

"It's what Walter made out of the People's Lumber Company—and more besides. Gouged here and there from Eunice and me. It makes things easy. One of us'll have to go settle with the Consolidated. I guess an audit of the books in Boston'll show how much is theirs. I want they should be paid every penny."

"I'll go," said Knuckles. "Um—what about the mill?"

They eyed each other in silence. "I can't run a mill," James said. "Not the business or the manufacturing end. It isn't my work. I couldn't bear bein' shut up. But ——"

"I could," said Knuckles. "Um—a Perrigo and

a Knuckles! . . . Manufacturin' end. . . . But there's Cross."

"I was thinking about him. How's he fixed?"

"No idea. But he'd be handy. Run the office and the sales and the business end. Maybe we could rig up a deal."

"We'll put it up to him. And anyhow you and I can go ahead and buy. . . . You better do the dickering."

"I'll go to New York tomorrow," Knuckles said.

"Maybe the Cross family won't want to stay here."

"One of 'em will," said Knuckles, with a brightness in his eye, "if I'm any judge."

"Sarah stays," said James. "We better get that trunk to the bank. . . . Um—here comes Eunice." He glanced sidewise at Knuckles. "I'm goin' to find Sarah."

Eunice flung out of the car and ran up the steps; at sight of Knuckles she paused and frowned.

"I'm keeping house," he said gravely. "Step right in."

"Ab," she said a little tremulously, "what is it all about? What does everything mean?" Her eyes opened wide. "Oh, there's the trunk."

"There's the trunk," he said flatly.

"And where—where is Walter?"

"Walter—Walter kind of decided to go away. Um—he won't be back. . . . You look here, Eunice, it's just as well if you don't know everything—mebby some better—so long's you know everythin's all right."

"Is it?"

"Yes."

"And James?"

"James and I," said Knuckles, "cal'late to be business partners. I don't know a man I'd trust farther than James."

"I'm so glad," she said, and dropped her eyes. "I —I wanted one honest brother."

A brief silence fell. Knuckles was searching for words, and words did not come easy to him. "You've always disliked me sort of special," he said.

"Well ——"

"And you've been plain-spoken about it."

"That was before ——" She lifted eyes, which for once were serious, neither reckless nor angry nor jeering.

"I never disliked you," said Knuckles.

"No?"

"I don't believe in goin' at a thing haphazard, nor slapdash."

"You wouldn't," she said, with a smile not innocent of mischief.

"That's why I'm kind of leadin' up."

"Leading up to what?"

"To askin' if I could come and see you."

"And call? You —— Why, yes."

"And take you out ridin'?"

She wrinkled her eyes and pursed her lips. "Ab Knuckles, what are you trying to get at?"

"What I'm gettin' at is," he said very awkwardly, indeed, "that I'd like to come pretty often, and all."

"You want to keep steady company with me?" she asked, her eyes overrunning with laughter.

"Somethin' like that."

She nodded. "Object matrimony?"

Knuckles' ears grew red and redder. "Wa-al, it's kind of premature to talk about that," he said, "but I own up it's what I had in mind."

She pretended to consider it judiciously. "I'll tell you," she said, "suppose you come around tonight and we'll try it out. And I'll go riding with you to-morrow."

"I got to go to New York," he interrupted.

"Then I won't go riding with you tomorrow, but when you can spare me the time."

He scented irony in this, but did not know exactly where it lay. "Why," he said, "I cal'late to spare you a lot of time—if you'll put up with me."

"Ab," she said, touching his sleeve lightly with her fingers, "something tells me I'm going to be able to put up with you quite comfortably. . . . And there's Sarah and James."

Warren Cross continued to improve rapidly; in a week he was allowed out for a drive, and his progress was made pleasant by the greetings of Colchester. People he did not know smiled at him pleasantly, mere acquaintances congratulated him and shook his hand. His appearance was a public event. He could not but be aware of the good will which showered upon him; nor could Janet, as she sat by his side.

"They act as if they were really glad to see me out," Warren said happily.

"They—everybody has been awfully kind."

"See the hills," he said, "with the sun on them. I can almost smell them. I wish I could drive near enough to the mill to smell sawdust."

"There's Henry Bridge. We must stop. He's ——I don't know what I'd have done without Kitty. And Henry's just living for the day when he can give you what he calls your coming-out party."

Warren smiled and shook his bandaged head. "Good folks. . . . Something about them." His voice dragged off into comfortable silence. Again and again Janet saw his eyes brighten as hands waved to him; there was Doc Lowrie and Mandy Hewitt and Larry Fox and fat old Mrs. Paget, whom he did not know at all, but who waved wildly a red parasol.

"Who's that?"

"Some kind of an aunt of our cook's," Janet said, with a smile which was not condescending. "Widow of the bank president."

"Gosh!" said Warren.

Presently they came home again, and saw on the front stoop James Perrigo and Knuckles, who arose

and came down to the car to open the door and help
Warren out.

"Old Doc said we could talk business today," said
Knuckles.

"The way I feel," said Warren, "you could talk
theosophy. Go ahead."

"It's about the mill," Knuckles said, when Warren
was made comfortable on the sofa. "Got any plans?"

Warren's face fell; he glanced at Janet and then
turned his eyes away. "I suppose I'll be going back.
The firm is holding my old job for me." He put on
a cheerful smile. "Yes, I'll be going back soon now.
Then you can ride all day on a Subway train, Janet."

"Um—James and I have bought the mill."

"No! I heard it was to be sold back. I'm glad—
that's fine."

"James'll run the woods end and I'm going to make
a fist of the manufacturing, but that kind of leaves
the office and sales and that part danglin'."

"Oh, you'll manage that."

"We thought maybe you'd manage that," said
Knuckles.

"Me?"

"To be sure. We don't want to pry into your
business any, but the three of us as partners, ownin'
share and share alike——"

"What?"

"Be good money in it for everybody. . . . But I
cal'late you'll be wantin' to get back to New York."

"But—a third share! How much? I haven't a

great deal of money—only twelve or fifteen thousand I've scrimped and saved."

"And that twenty-five thousand of mine," said Janet, and bit her lip.

"What?"

"Let's see. That's forty thousand. Um—balance could be fixed up at the bank, all right. But, as you say, you don't want to stay here——"

Warren looked at Janet and as quickly withdrew his eyes. She stood up and walked to Warren's side and let her hand touch his forehead. "I—I don't want to go back," she said. "I—I want to stay here." Warren moistened his lips and stared. "I ——Oh, there's Aunt Hat and the Old Doc and— and Kitty and Edna Fox and—and everybody that kept sending in things and being so—so good. They're all here. And if we went back there wouldn't be—be anybody but ambulances and—and hospitals like barracks and cut flowers with a card in the box! I—I don't care what anybody says—I don't care— I want to stay here!"

Warren's eyes glowed; he lifted himself on his elbow and his face was radiant. "But the theaters and the shops and—and everything."

"I—I want to stay here," Janet said, and then added another phrase: "With folks."

Warren was erect now. "Boys," he said eagerly— "boys, if we can pull it off—if the bank is willing— it's a deal."

James spoke for the first time. "Kind of a family

deal," he said diffidently. "There's Sarah and I ——"

"What?"

"Sarah was—was goin' to stay here anyhow," he said.

"I'll—be—darned! Sarah of all folks!" He waggled his head. "She's a—a flapper!"

James' brown eyes twinkled. "And Knuckles here—he's hangin' around our front stoop so much I use the back door. And Eunice don't even make a motion to drive him off."

"Gcsh," said Warren, "what a set of brothers-in-law!"

Knuckles cleared his throat. "Um," he said, and then, resembling his father in that his lips scarcely moved as he spoke: "This all's come out full better'n I looked for in the commencement."

(THE END)